TRANSMISSION

TRANSMISSION

SAMANTHA ARTHURS

Cat & Key Books
Philadelphia

This is a work of fiction. Names and places are imaginary or used fictitiously. Any resemblance to real places or persons is a matter of coincidence.

Cat & Key Books
PHILADELPHIA

ISBN 978-1-955646-05-5 (hardback)
ISBN 978-1-955646-03-1 (paperback)
ISBN 978-1-955646-04-8 (ebook)

TRANSMISSION
Copyright © 2021 by Samantha Arthurs

Book design by Michael Knightley

All rights reserved.
No part of this book may be used or reproduced in any manner without written permission of the author, except as brief excerpts in reviews or as permitted by the U.S. Copyright Act of 1976.

First Electronic Edition, September 2021
First Paperback Edition, September 2021

*No one can tell what goes
on in between the person you were and
the person you become.*

- Stephen King
The Stand

For Mrs. Lee, who was the first teacher to encourage me as a writer. Without you, I wouldn't have written any of these words.

For Carolyn, who loved that old brickyard and taught me all about the place I would later fictionalize as Graven. Thank you for the stories.

You are both missed.

This one is for the 41142-73-64, and the whole 606.

ONE

THE WORLD WAS NOW A QUIET PLACE, BUT IT hadn't always been that way. Less than a year ago the world had been filled with the steady buzz of electricity, the muted conversations from the television, and the honk of car horns and the revving of engines. Now there were only the whispers of nature, the sounds that most had rarely taken the time to notice until that was all there was. Instead of the sounds of the modern world there was just the faint hiss of the wind blowing through trees, water flowing over rocks, and animals prowling through underbrush. Sounds that had become more prominent and were brought to the foreground when everything else had fallen away.

Seventeen-year-old Avery Harris had never thought much about the way the world sounded until the day the power had finally gone out five months previous. The hum of the lights had been his last and final tie to the old world, save for the static of the radio that he could never get tuned into anything substantial. He had missed it at first, the sounds of the power moving through the lines, but as with everything else that had happened he moved on quickly. There was no choice anymore but to move on, to see what was going to happen next.

The unincorporated town, if you could call it that, of Graven was located about three miles off the main road, which wasn't saying much since the main road wasn't anything to write home about either. There wasn't a lot to Graven or the nearby town of Carter Springs, which at least had a leg up because it was on the map and had a town government. Carter Springs also boasted a couple of gas stations, a grocery store, and a bank. That was all there was to it, but Avery had always been happy enough. Small town life had suited him, but that was when he had a family to fall back on.

Back before loneliness had become his only friend and ally.

He sat now in the shadowy old post office he called home, bundled inside a couple of heavy blankets he'd lifted from a nearby house. He was eating pickled sausages out of a plastic jar, pausing every few bites to give one to Tilly, his beagle, and only other surviving family member. He'd brought her with him after leaving the sick house, craving companionship and feeling a sense of duty to her. He had raised her from a pup, and he would not abandon her now even when the world was crumbling around them.

"We'll go out tomorrow," he promised her, ruffling her long, floppy ears. "You need more kibble, and I want to keep stockpiling. Winter is coming fast; we don't want to be stuck here without enough supplies to get us through. Talk about the very worst-case scenario there is."

Tilly licked his hand and wagged her tail, not understanding a word he said but pleased with the head scratches. She left him then, going to her bed under the heavy old desk he'd shoved against one of the doors where she promptly fell asleep. Avery didn't rest yet though, consumed by all he had to do before it got cold and snowy, and by all that had already happened. Two years ago, a Louisiana pig farmer had gotten sick, and the rest of the country had followed him into the dark.

The world didn't end quickly, the way that it does in movies. No, it happened much slower than that and lasted, give or take, about two years before it was all over. If you asked Avery Harris what he thought about it, well, he was apt to tell you it felt both faster and slower than any amount of time had ever felt before. There isn't anyone left around to ask him though, because he is the last one.

He had read enough books and watched enough television to know how it was supposed to be in fantasy and exactly how it wasn't in reality. Fiction always had the protagonist finding other survivors. They always banded together to take out the baddies who were still lurking in all the dark and gloomy places. So far, Avery hadn't seen anyone, good or bad, in seven months. That was when his mother had succumbed, and he had become the sole population of Graven, Kentucky. He was the last human standing in this remote corner of nowhere, and possibly even in the entire state. Or, realistically, maybe even in the entire country or the world.

According to the last reports coming in off the television and radio, the virus had spread from North America. The television had gone out sometime in May, and the radio had finally given up the ghost in early July. The last transmissions told that cases had cropped up in London, Paris, Rome, and as far away as Moscow, Beijing, and Tokyo. It seemed that there wasn't anywhere left untouched by the Ruger Virus, named for the doctor at the CDC who had discovered it. At first, it was believed to be a strange mutation of the flu, but that had been so wrong. Not only had it been wrong, but it was a mistake that ultimately proved to be deadly. By the time they figured it out, thousands of people were down with it, confined to their homes and beds, and unknowingly spreading it to their friends and loved ones.

There was no cure. There was no vaccine. Within two years, the population of the world had dwindled. In those two years, Avery Harris became the last living person that he knew of. It was a heavy burden to carry, being the last of something, especially the last of something as immense as the human race. Logically he knew that he probably wasn't the only one left, but until he met another it was a safe enough conclusion to make.

It had first cropped up in Louisiana, in a pig farmer who came down with the sweats, the shakes, and a nasty cough. The doctor had given him a prescription for Tamiflu and told him to get plenty of rest and to get his flu shot next year. Only the man, named Benny Robichaud, never made it to next year. In fact, he never made it to next Tuesday. By that Sunday, his liver had swollen considerably, and he was coughing up blood. He died quickly after a violent seizure like episode, and that was that. They buried Benny in the local cemetery; then sent someone out to check out the pigs.

If not the flu, then maybe something viral he caught from the animals. It happened all the time, right? The pigs all checked out healthy, as far as pigs go anyway, and life went on. Benny

Robichaud was considered a fluke, a medical mystery, and another blip on the nightly news when all was said and done.

Until his wife came down with it a few days later, followed quickly by several members of his local congregation, a nearby farmer friend, and his family physician. All of them had the same symptoms, and all were dead within days. It was spreading, and so was the fear that came along with it. People rushed out for vaccinations and over the counter medications, flooding doctors' offices if they so much as spiked a tiny fever. That was part of how and why it spread so fast, people flocking together in tight quarters when they should have been staying home and avoiding contact.

Within just a few weeks it had crept into the surrounding states, cases showing up all over the United States. Air travel became restricted in an effort to keep the disease contained, but people tried to get out anyway. They ran across the borders into Mexico and Canada, carrying their germs on their backs. It wasn't long before cases showed up there as well, and once it hit low-income areas it was like throwing a match into a barrel full of gasoline.

It didn't matter though, not in the end. The Ruger virus didn't care if you were rich or poor; it hit everyone the same way. Nursing homes and long-term care facilities went first, completely decimating the patients and the staff members alike. Then it started ravaging hospitals, jumping from one patient to another, spreading to nurses, doctors, interns, and janitors. Eventually health care facilities began closing their doors, and doctors refused to see patients with Ruger symptoms. There was nothing to do for them but send them home to die; no treatment exists to even prolong life once diagnosed.

Avery finished his dinner and put the remaining sausages back on the shelf. Tomorrow he would do a supply count before a run into town, but for now, he needed to sleep. He checked the doors one more time, and then checked that the windows were all well covered. He got another blanket, not willing yet to waste any of his resources on heat just yet and curled up on the air mattress he had tucked into the corner. It was hard to get good rest when everything was so quiet, and his mind was racing, waiting for the other shoe to fall. Waiting to get sick, for someone to come, for something else bad to happen. Nothing truly positive had happened for two years, so he didn't know what else to expect anymore. Surely, probably, nothing good.

TWO

GRAVEN HAD A POST OFFICE, HOUSED INSIDE OF AN old building that had belonged to the brickyard just up the road. It was a drafty, creaking sort of place that had constantly been on the verge of being closed down for one reason or another. He could remember two summers previous when the ceiling had caved in, and everyone had been sure that was the end of it. Only it hadn't been, and he was grateful for that now. The brickyard company had repaired the roof, laid in new pipes, and had even replaced the gas furnace not so long ago. That furnace was one of Avery's primary reasons for choosing the place as his new home base, a wise decision if he had ever had one.

He had spent his entire life in Graven, living just past the bridge you had to cross to reach the post office itself. His childhood home had been simple place, a small white house with three upstairs bedrooms and a modest living space and kitchen downstairs. It had sat perched on the hillside, and you had to park at the bottom and climb a set of seven steps to reach the front porch. It had been treacherous in bad weather, but they had made it work just the same. Avery had never imagined he would live anywhere else, he hadn't been old enough to imagine that yet, but after his mother had died he knew he had to get out. Escape had been partially for his own sanity; and also a need to get away from the germs. If he wasn't yet infected, which seemed unlikely, he didn't want to risk further exposure.

So, he had burned the place down, keeping vigil all night to make sure the flames didn't engulf everything else in the area. As the fire had burned down, he had taken his few worldly possession and crossed the bridge to the post office, curious about the building and whether or not it might be beneficial for him in anyway. He'd forced open the back door, and had found something more perfect than he could have imagined.

The old building had a gas furnace, and more than that the large tank outside was full which meant he could have heat all winter long and maybe beyond if he didn't squander it and was resourceful. The mail boxes were all empty and gathering dust, but they had a lot of promise. They would be a nice way to organize small items, like first aid supplies and tools. There was also a tall table with more little boxes above it, though he had no idea what its original use may have been. He saw it now as a place to store canned food and a prep area for meals. He could store the few things he'd taken from the house before it had burned in the safe, which was an amusing thought. They weren't worth anything besides emotional value, and it wasn't as though there was anyone around to steal. The thought just gave him comfort, and that was something he desperately needed.

Below the building was a narrow cellar type space, where he might be able to store fruits and vegetables if he could get ahold of any, and the bathroom had a toilet that would flush fine with water put in the tank. That was a good thing, because he did have plenty of water. The office sat right up against a wide creek that was constantly flowing with rusty-colored water. He knew that was due to minerals of some kind, and he resolved to just boil anything before drinking it to be on the safe side.

His discovery of the post office had all happened months ago now, and he was well set up inside with everything he was going to need and then some. He had brought a fire pit over from a neighbor's backyard, setting it up right outside the back door. It was out there that he built small fires every day to boil water and to cook on. He spent the past few weeks driving an old pickup truck along all the nearby roads, gathering up wood from people's back porches and sheds. He now had a substantial stack of it between the door and the old drop off box outside, covered with a tarp to keep it as dry as he could.

The food supply wasn't bad either. So many canned and boxed goods filled the little cubbies and overflowed into the cabinets and drawers. He had picked up a small heater on another outing, along with a whole box of small gas tanks for it. It was an emergency backup plan, should anything happen to the furnace. He'd gotten tools to repair things, and several different kinds of lanterns that ran on everything from propane tanks to batteries. He had plenty of those too, every size and type stuffed into the old mailboxes that had been repurposed to hold his inventory.

Now Avery was making a list, standing at the counter with the little window up so he could see into the lobby area. In here, he stored a bicycle, dog food for Tilly, bottles, and jugs of water to be used when the culvert potentially froze over, fishing gear, and clothes. He looked over all the items and made a few more notes on his list, looking down at the beagle who was staring up at him with intense interest.

"You know we're going for a ride, huh?" Avery asked Tilly with a smile, reaching into his pocket to fish out a treat. He gave her one and then made a note to try and find some more, letting out a heavy breath as he read back over everything. "I need to try and find a good coat today, and a new pair of gloves and a hat. Socks, we need more socks, and I want to get some more blankets too because you can never have too many of those. We found that shotgun two weeks ago at the Johnson's, remember? Maybe we can find shells for it today, which will be good to have. Maybe we can hunt some this winter, try and have some fresh meat. We mostly we need to look for medicine, especially cold meds, cough syrup, and stuff. It's going to get colder, and neither of us can afford for me to get down sick."

Tilly stared at him like she understood, tilting her head to one side. She was angling for another treat but knew better than to beg, settling for wagging her tail and stretching out so her paws bumped against his shoe. Avery wasn't even paying attention anymore, sliding the list into his back pocket before tugging on his jacket. He grabbed the car keys off the peg board by the door and then opened the back door, letting the dog run out ahead of him. He paused to lock the door tight with a padlock he'd gotten after a trip to the hardware store, making sure everything was secure before they set out. His worst fear was that there was someone lurking around, and that they'd snag up all of his hard work while he wasn't there to defend it.

The beagle was already at the car, doing a little tap dance around it and letting out a single bay. That made Avery smile as he opened up the driver's side door, letting her jump in first. The car was a Camaro, shiny blue with dark windows that he had liberated from another nearby house. He'd driven the truck until it had run out of gas, and before that, it had been a Jeep. Playing musical vehicles was easier than trying to steal gas, a bridge that he would cross whenever he got there. For now though he only made the short trip into town or to the gas stations out by the interstate, so that made it far less of a concern at the moment.

One of the few perks of being the only person left standing was that nobody was around to see you breaking the law. When Avery took off, squealing tires with the windows down, nobody was there to chastise him. He blew through both stop signs and took the curves at a clip, Tilly slipping and sliding all over the seat beside him. The reckless driving, being the only human being on the road, was one of the few things that Avery took real pleasure in. He even turned on the radio and pushed play on the iPod he'd found in the glove compartment, loud rock music blaring out. What was the purpose of living in an empty world if you didn't at least do a few of the things you had always wanted to do? Sure, it wasn't traveling to Europe or standing on the edge of the Grand Canyon, but it was what he had, and he was going to enjoy it.

Once on the main road, Avery exercised a little bit more caution. Most of that was owing to the fact that the main road wasn't fully clear, and he had to take care to move around several accidents on the way into town. The worst was an overturned big rig right at the bridge that you had to cross to get into town. It had jackknifed, covering both lanes almost entirely. The left lane had just enough clearance left to squeak past the tilted trailer if you dropped off the edge and into the grass, creeping back onto the pavement just as the bank gave way to the corner of the bridge. From there it was smaller things, like two t-boned cars in front of the middle school, and a mess of bricks slung all over the place somehow. There was broken glass and garbage too, papers and plastic bags floating listlessly in the wind.

This was what he had imagined the apocalypse might look like; because this was what it always looked like on television. It was apparently the one thing that writers and directors had gotten right when trying to bring the vision to life. At the end of the world, when desolation and isolation set in and there was nothing left, places that had once been prosperous and familiar became scary ghost towns fraught with harrowing imagery.

Once he made it into town he parked the car in the parking lot of the grocery store first, fishing around in the small backseat for what he would need. He got out the crowbar, a hammer, and a box of nails which he slid into his pockets and the belt loops of his jeans. He grabbed several reusable grocery bags, better for carrying things because they were more heavy-duty, and then he and Tilly set out. Instead of using the front doors, which were held tightly closed with chains and a heavy lock, he went around to the side door. It was boarded shut with thick nails and a piece of plywood, which he had put up last time he'd gone on a run. It was more to keep out animals than to dissuade any other potential human beings, easy to pry loose once he got the crowbar in place. It was quick work, and then the plywood hit the ground, Avery shoving open the door. He let Tilly run in ahead, not needing a flashlight since he wasn't going anywhere in the back of the store.

There were high windows along the front of the store that let in enough autumn sunlight that he could see just fine. He consulted his list and got what he thought he would need, including candles, matches, and some more canned stuff. He found a bag of marshmallows he had overlooked last time, and two canned hams that he knew would look disgusting but would state fine enough with the right kind of love. He got some sodas and bottles of Gatorade, which could be kept cold in the space beneath the building, and all the pain killers left on the shelves. There wasn't a lot, but he would take whatever he could find. He'd been in this store several times now, and each time he found one or two things he had overlooked though he knew that, sooner rather than later, there would be nothing left to find.

It was a shame too; all the stuff that could have been used, but that was now well past that point. The first time he'd come into the store, he'd hardly been able to stand it, the sweet smell of rotting meat, fruits, and vegetables turning his stomach. There were bins, coolers, and boxes full of stuff that had turned already, along with plenty of items on the shelves. The breads, buns, and deli items were long gone, though he had managed to score some packaged snack cakes that came individually wrapped. Those had gotten stale but were still edible.

Finishing up in the store, Avery boarded the door again out of habit and loaded up the narrow trunk of the car. He called to Tilly, who came running, and they hopped back inside together. He had two more stops to make, and one of them was more important than perhaps even the grocery store. He had to get into the pharmacy again, and this time he had to get to the prescription stuff. He needed cold medications, cough remedies, and pain medications. Things that he might never use, but that he didn't want to risk not having on hand should the need arise. He'd already gotten all the first aid supplies he could handle off the front of store shelves and had secured quite a lot of over-the-counter things. What he needed now was the good stuff, locked away behind the bars that covered the windows and doors of the back area. He needed the stuff that was protected and kept secure and the stuff that could mean life or death if he got truly sick or hurt.

This meant he had to make one last run to the hardware store too, which was just as well. He was out now, and it would be a waste of gas to just grab a few meager groceries and go back. Not to mention he wanted to scout out a few houses he hadn't been to yet, in hopes of finding shells for the gun and maybe other useful materials.

Navigating through the desolate town made Avery's already heavy heart sink further, seeing all of the places that had once been so familiar to him and so full of life. He thought about the people who had populated the place, all those faces he had known for all his life, and now they were just gone. As he edged along around a toppled lamp post, he let himself remember, thinking back to when it had started and how stupidly naïve they had all been.

THREE

August 2017 – The arrival of Ruger

"STOP IT, JESSA, I MEAN IT! IF YOU DON'T QUIT IT, then I'm going to tell mom!"

The Harris house was full of noise and activity, which was fairly par for the course on a humid Saturday afternoon. It was too hot to do much of anything outside besides sweat, although the house would start to feel incredibly small if you stayed inside for too long with all four family members, plus the dog, present at the same time. There was no hard win-win to this particular situation, and there likely wouldn't be for another week or two until the temperatures began to cool off, and it was once again comfortable to be outdoors during daylight hours.

School had started back the previous week, and Avery, now fifteen years old, was already busy with homework and high school drama while Jessa, eight on the cusp of nine, took great pleasure in tormenting him every chance she got. She was just at that age where being a pest was a fun way to pass the time, and it drove poor Avery absolutely mad. Their parents encouraged him to have patience with her, and at worst just try to ignore her all together when she got into those sorts of moods. It was incredibly hard, however, and he sometimes cracked despite his best efforts.

Breakfast was long since over, and they were now hovering near the lunch hour. Avery had set himself up in the cool living room, where the large window unit air conditioner was chugging out blissful cold air that just barely combated the heat of the day. He'd spread his math homework out over the coffee table, and he sat on the floor hunched over it with the eraser of his pencil in his mouth. Jessa kept on hovering over him, flailing and bouncing and being a general distraction. He had begged her repeatedly to stop, and the longer it went on the shriller he became.

Jemma, their mother, was in the kitchen with the dishwasher running and beans on to cook for dinner. She had laid out sandwich fixings for lunch, and was working on kneading bread dough while the radio droned on from the corner of the counter. She was considering going into the living room herself to finally get Jessa out of her brother's hair when something on the radio caught her attention, and she paused everything else to listen.

"....five new cases in Kentucky in the past two days....urging people to stay indoors, especially those presenting symptoms....Louisiana....no known cure, still unidentified at the time of this broadcast..."

For a couple of weeks now, there had been murmurings of a new super-flu going around, and reportedly several people had died from it. The news tried to make it appear as though it were no big deal and that relatively healthy people were fine, but the scientific community wasn't buying that at all. They were urging people to act with caution, to limit their contact with others until they figured out exactly what the virus, if it was a virus, was and what the root cause was.

It hadn't seemed immediately concerning; most things weren't, but more and more cases cropped up with each passing week. It had reached Kentucky days ago now which meant it was really spreading, no longer contained to the starting point of Louisiana. Five new cases in just two days, though? That was pretty bad, and Jemma found herself drying her hands on a dish towel and approaching the living room after all.

"Jessa, sit down. Leave him alone," she snapped at her daughter as she turned on the television, seeking out the televised noon broadcast of the local news. She found the station and then sat down on the sofa beside where Avery was working, focusing on the program.

The headline was right at the top of the screen, and she knew it had caught the attention of the children too because they not only went silent, they also went very still. Jessa was now perched on the edge of the armchair, eyes fixated on the screen, while Avery stared ahead with the eraser still clenched between his teeth.

"Mystery virus claims more lives," Avery read out loud, voice barely above a whisper as he spoke. "Is that the same thing that killed that farmer in Louisiana?"

"Shh, just listen," Jemma whispered to him, resting a hand in his dirty blond hair as they watched the program.

Five people had indeed come down with the sickness in the past two days, confirmed by the University of Kentucky hospital, and one of them had already died. That was on top of four others who had died in Louisville during the course of the week, and two more in Hazard. Those were three separate places, with quite a few miles between each of them. The two in Hazard had recently returned from a trip to Florida, while one of the folks in Louisville had been a nurse at the Jewish hospital. Two more had been teachers, and another a social worker. They all had different professions, had been in very different circumstances, but all of them had come down with the very same thing that had indeed killed the farmer from Louisiana.

At first everyone had been under the impression that the man from Haughton, Louisiana, named Benny Robichaud, had contracted some sort of disease from the pigs on his farm. All of the animals had checked out though, not a single one presenting any unusual symptoms or signs of illness. Blood tests of several animals had proven that they were indeed healthy, they weren't carrying whatever had offed Benny, and so doctors had started looking elsewhere for the answer. It was just a few days after Benny had died that his wife also fell ill with the same symptoms, and then other members of their local community became ill as well. All of them had eventually died, and they were still no closer to an answer about where the sickness had come from or what the cause was.

On the television the pretty female newscaster, who was usually seen with a wide smile on her face, looked incredibly somber. She shuffled her notes, eyes finally meeting the camera as she began to speak again.

"High fever, cough with bloody discharge, accelerated heart rate, cold sweats, and headaches. If you have any combination of these symptoms, doctors are encouraging you to stay home and quarantine yourself if possible. If your condition worsens, please call the number below to speak to a physician directly. Anyone who has come into direct contact with someone presenting these symptoms, you are asked to likewise quarantine yourself and avoid contact with others. It can take up to three days for the illness to incubate and for symptoms to begin. As of the time of this broadcast, local emergency rooms are at capacity, and are turning away anyone who does not need immediate critical care. Please, stay home. To avoid becoming infected, and to avoid potentially infecting others."

It was such a weird thing, like something straight out of a movie. It reminded Avery of what might have happened on a zombie television program, something that took place at the very beginning when people first started to reanimate after death. They all fell ill from a mysterious sickness, and then just a couple of days later, the world was overrun with the living dead. It made him shiver a bit, finally taking the pencil out of his mouth. He turned sideways to look up at his mom, his green eyes wide with shock.

"This sounds pretty serious," he told her, brushing his hair back off his forehead. "Do you think dad knows about this?"

Telford Harris, the patriarch and sole breadwinner of the family, worked driving a truck for a local company that specialized in fill dirt, gravel, and rocks. While he didn't come into contact with mass groups of people he was still out there, conversing and congregating with all different sorts of folks every single day. It made Avery feel nervous inside, shifting his weight a little, pulling one leg up, and hugging it to his chest with both arms wrapped around it.

"I think dad is probably just fine," Jemma told him, careful not to give total assurance or a promise with her words. She didn't know if he was truly fine or not; she was just hopeful that he likely was at least for the moment. "Ave, why don't you put your shoes on? You and me can make a run to the store. Jessa, don't even ask. The answer is no. I want you to stay here and make sure the beans don't burn."

The real reason Jemma wanted Jessa to stay behind was not to mind the beans, but to stay away from anyone who might be sick. There was no real correlation thus far to the illness and age, but it was a known fact that the very old and the relatively young tended to be more susceptible to anything coming and going, so it was better for the youngest to stay behind. Not to mention she tended to get underfoot, and this trip needed to be quick. Just a little stock up on the essentials and maybe some bottled water, just in case.

Jemma and Avery left the house, and a pouting Jessa, behind to head into town. Normally things were relatively busy on a Saturday, and while there were people out and about they had both expected more than this. Nobody seemed to put out or harried, everyone going about their normal Saturday afternoon routines. They went to the grocery store on the far side of town, the cheaper one that sat at the top of the hill near the Dairy Queen. The shelves were fairly empty, but that wasn't an unusual thing. Cheaper did not always mean well-stocked, though they had everything on the small list that Jemma had made.

They got two cases of bottled water, some canned goods, a couple of loaves of bread, and a fresh gallon of milk. They stocked up on batteries for flashlights, a couple of small canisters of charcoal lighter for the grill, and an entire bushel of apples that Avery knew they'd never eat and would probably have to slice and freeze for some other purpose.

The pair didn't run into anyone they knew until they got into the checkout lane, where Jacob Flannery was unloading enough frozen meals onto the conveyor belt to last him through this winter and the next. He grinned at Jemma when he saw her behind him, holding up a stack of paper in his hands.

"Coupons," he told her, handing those over to the cashier, who was still ringing up the meals at an excruciatingly slow pace. "Hell of a good deal! What are you two up to today? Been awhile since I've seen you, Avery! You goin' out for the football team this year?"

Avery, who had never played football in his life, shook his head and offered Jacob a small smile. His dad had grown up with Jacob Flannery, had graduated high school with him, so while he was always baffled at the man's insistence that he was an athlete, he always spared him a kind word in return.

"Nah, no football for me, too busy with studying and everything else. Did you see the news? About everybody starting to get sick? Mom thought we should get some things from the store, just in case they get more serious about people staying inside," he explained, drumming his fingers on the handle of the cart. "You sure you just want to buy T.V. dinners?"

It was now Jacob's turn to look a little confused, opening his wallet as the cashier finally began to scan his coupons. "You mean that virus that guy from way down south got? Aw, c'mon, ya'll can't really believe that stuff, right? That's just what the media wants us to think, that everybody around here is gonna come down with that. Look at where we live! You really think some big disease is going to spread all the way to nowhere like this? Everybody who has got sick around here is either from a city, or was away visitin' somewhere else. Them people down in Hazard, they didn't get sick at home. They brought it back from Disney World! They just want us to worry, so we do stuff like that, run out and buy all sorts of stuff we don't even need. Nobody is getting sick; mark it down, so you remember I was the first to tell you."

It was clear from the look on Jemma's face that she was frustrated with Jacob, and with his potentially very false information. It wasn't the first, or last, time they would hear such a declaration however. A lot of people would presume that such a sickness would never spread to somewhere so rural, and that as long as you stuck to your small town and avoided big cities and traveling too far away that you'd be just fine. Avery knew that a mentality like that could be deadly, and he knew that every single person was at risk the moment they set foot out of the house. He didn't keep contradicting people though, and he took every single crackpot theory as they came.

With time they would hear everything from the virus being avian and spread by birds, to being spread across the entire world via contaminated waterways. The fear of something brought out the worst in humanity as a general rule, and Avery Harris learned that lesson on that very first day, right there at the local discount grocery store.

Later that evening, after his homework was done and the dinner dishes drying in the rack, the family gathered around the television again. This time his father was included, four somber faces listening to the latest updates and watching interviews from doctors across the country. The advice was by and large the same, just try to stay indoors and away from anyone who might be sick, making it the country's sickest waiting game. Wait to find out if everyone around you got sick, waiting to see if you managed to avoid it or not.

Most people wouldn't. That much became apparent very, very quickly.

FOUR

AVERY PULLED INTO THE PARKING LOT THAT WAS just off the main street, right beside the hardware store and across the street from the old pharmacy. He had already been to the other pharmacy in town and had found it fairly empty, likely looted by the owners and staff before they had left. Rose's Pharmacy, though, was a hometown staple, and they had stayed open as long as they could before being forced to finally shut down. If Mr. Rose hadn't fallen ill, they probably would have managed even longer, but once he got down with the Ruger virus, they had locked it up and it had sat there lonely and desolate ever since.

He had been in and out a couple of times already for small things, but today's haul was going to be a big one. He had to start at the hardware store first though, hopping out of the car with Tilly on his heels. He didn't have to pry the door open this time; he just pushed it and let himself in, the bell jingling overhead like some sort of ancient relic. It made him smile a little though to hear that faint sound that was so well associated with live before the plague.

Opening the bag he'd thrown over his shoulder, Avery began to browse the aisles, picking up small things that could prove useful later. Screws and nails, things to fix common plumbing issues, and all the remaining matches and lighters he could get his hands on. He grabbed duct tape and some more small propane tanks, and then he found what he had purposefully come for.

It was a small hand-held blow torch, the kind that ran on a small tank of gas. He got the tank for it too and paused for a moment to read the instructions. The last thing he wanted, or needed, was to blow himself up or sustain some sort of burns on his body. He tried to be careful about injuries, because infection was a very real thing and even with medicine it could potentially kill him. It would be a shame to live through a global pandemic only to die from a cut on the palm of your hand.

Dropping the torch into the bag, he then zipped it shut, whistling for his dog. They left the store together and crossed the street to the pharmacy; this door was also left standing open. He had cleared out what food had been here ages ago, so he didn't worry about animals getting inside like he had at the grocery store. In fact, most of the front shelves were totally bare, safe for things like tampons and condoms, all things he did not have a use for. What he wanted today was in the back, locked up tight behind one of those roll down windows made of metal that was used to deter thieves. That was where the torch would come in, his last-ditch effort to get to the stuff that was kept out of the public eye.

He had already considered coming in through the back of the building, but it was not the best laid plan. The backdoor was entered through a narrow alley with a tall gate locked from the alley side with a heavy padlock. He had climbed a ladder to peek over, noting that the door was also locked with a deadbolt, and possibly another padlock on the inside. He just didn't see himself able to get inside, as disheartening as it had been, and had instead spent a few weeks working on a secondary plan. The torch was his best and only hope, the only thing he'd come up with besides trying to drive a vehicle through the building itself. That was not promising at all, the probability of injury was too great, so this would be his only real shot.

Once they were inside the main area of the pharmacy, Avery set to work, opening his bag and taking out his supplies. Tilly did her part by sniffing around under shelves, chasing out mice and other small critters that had started to take over. She cowered though when he turned on the torch, the hissing of the flame spooking her enough that she slunk behind the counter to hide out until it was over.

Avery had anticipated that cutting through the bars would be easy; it always was on television after all, but he was in for a rude awakening. The metal was more durable than he had imagined, and the torch less powerful. He used up almost the entire tank of gas, cutting through just one side, and by that point he was tired and ready for a bit of a break. He rested on the floor, munching on a protein bar he'd put into the bag before leaving. After getting back a bit of energy he started on the other side and ended up having to cross the street to fetch another tank for the torch.

Eventually, his hands and arms tired and his eyes watering from looking at the flame, the bars were weak enough for Avery to push them free. They fell back with a clatter that echoed off the walls, Tilly scuttling further back beneath the desk at the loud noise. He was in though, finally, and Avery grinned broadly as he surveyed what was behind the pharmacy window.

"Jackpot," he cried out, throwing his tired arms over his head in triumph. Celebrating could come later though, it was getting later, and he didn't really fancy being out after dark fell. He had no real explanation for that. There was most certainly nothing in the dark that didn't exist in the daylight, but it felt more isolated and spookier at night, and that was all the reasoning he needed.

Sliding over the counter after grabbing his duffel, Avery began browsing through the medicines. He knew what some of them were, making sure to snag plenty of antibiotics and different pain medications. He took other things too, like topical ointments for pain and itch relief and bottles of prescription-grade cough and cold meds. He found allergy medication for the spring, and pills that could help him sleep on those nights that he couldn't shut his mind off to rest. It was a bit like being a kid in a candy store, if candy had the power to heal you.

While he was there, he stocked up on more bandages and even a small suture kit he found under the counter. The duffel bag was bulging but he managed to zip it shut, shoving it over the counter first before he eased himself out. He whistled for Tilly, and together they left with their spoils, loading the backseat up.

"Just one more stop or two," Avery told the beagle who was sprawled out across the passenger seat. "We need shells for the shotgun, so we're going to have to brave a few houses. Hopefully we get lucky on the first try. That would be nice wouldn't it?"

The sky had grown cloudy while he'd raided the pharmacy, a chill in the air that hadn't quite been there before. He knew that winter was descending upon him *fast*, and that he likely wasn't far out from at least the first signs of snow. It made him shiver just to imagine it, easing the car down the street and then to the right, up a narrow road that led to a residential area with a lot of houses sitting close together. He hadn't been here before, he hadn't had a reason to be before, but he did now. They needed proper weapons, because at some point he would possibly have to hunt for food, and he didn't want to wait until that moment came up to try and scramble for what he needed.

His dad had never been a guy to own any kind of fancy weapons, keeping an old hand gun around the house for protection and one solitary shotgun. The only times Avery had ever used a weapon were with his grandfather, who took him turkey hunting a time or two and had taught him to use both a gun and a compound bow. He wasn't especially skilled with either, but he was hopeful that he could keep both himself and Tilly from starving if he had to. Which, he had to admit, was a time that didn't linger too far ahead in the future.

Parking in the middle of the street, Avery hopped out and surveyed the landscape. All the lawns were overgrown with weeds and wild flowers, most of which were long since dead and dried up. A few houses sported cars in the driveways, while others had been boarded up as though plywood and nails could keep Ruger out. Ultimately, he chose a place to the left, where a big pickup truck with a tool box sat parked on the lawn. It felt like a promising choice, and he grabbed his crowbar before making his way to the front door.

He was pleased to find the door unlocked, but less pleased to find that the place had been cleared out. It was very likely that the owners had packed up another vehicle and had left town to try and outrun the possibility of sickness, cleaning out everything from dresser drawers to a huge gun safe that sat completely empty. All he found of use were three cans of chili in the cabinet, which he tucked into the reusable grocery sack over his shoulder before heading back out to the street.

Avery had to bust out a window at the next house, where he had slightly better luck inside. He found a few shells for the shot gun, as well as a couple of hunting knives that would come in handy. The kitchen cabinets were empty though, just some rotting stuff in the fridge, and so he moved on yet again.

House three was by far and large the worst of the lot. It sat at the end of the cul-de-sac, a wind chime tinkling out a pretty melody as he approached. A large SUV and a small Geo sat side by side under the carport, the front door sitting partially open. He nudged it open slowly and stepped in, overwhelmed immediately by the scent of rot. He pulled his shirt up over his face and shooed Tilly back outside as he crept in further, pausing to gag and struggling to hold down the protein bar he'd just eaten.

Once he felt a bit more under control, he kept moving, peering into rooms. He found the couple, along with two small children, inside of what was presumably the master bedroom. The woman and the kids were laying on the bed, covered up to their necks with a sheet, and the man sat slumped on the floor with a gun resting between his knees. The gun was a shot gun, similar to the one Avery had, and where there was a gun, there was ammunition to be found.

Despite the churning of his stomach, Avery searched, opening and closing drawers and being careful not to disturb the bodies. He tried the closet next and was surprised to find a couple of boxes of shells hidden on the top shelf. He took them all; he would count them later, hurrying out as fast as he could go. He shut the door behind him on the way, tugging it shut before he stumbled to the edge of the porch. He finally threw up then, mostly just dry heaving and gagging. Tilly sat and watched him, whining in sympathy as he leaned against a porch post to steady himself.

"It's never going to get easier, is it girl?" He asked the dog, reaching down to pet her head before moving back toward the car. It didn't matter how many bodies you saw, it didn't matter how long you'd been living in such an empty world. It never got any better or easier. It was still horrible and horrifying, and it still made him feel sick to his stomach. He had lived and they hadn't, and it would never be entirely logical to him. It would never make one lick of sense why he hadn't gotten sick, why everyone around him had perished, but he had to go on living.

Avery had felt victory over his successful run, but now he just felt drained. He tossed the bag into the back with the other spoils, turning around slowly to make his way back to Graven. The wind had picked up now, he could feel it pushing against the car, and he let out a heavy sigh. He didn't have time to think about his own mortality, to consider why he had stayed healthy and hadn't come down with the fever and sickness like the rest had. Perhaps once winter was behind him, when things were better, he could consider it. For now, though, he had to keep facing down survival in an attempt to just make it to the other side.

He was on his way out, starting back along the winding road that would take him back to Main Street, when his eyes lit on a building he had never even considered before. The old high school was tall and imposing, a massive brick structure that sat atop the hill overlooking the town below. It hadn't been operational in a lot of years now, not since the mid 1970's, and a lot of the building was just sitting empty. However, the town library was located on the top floor and it struck him then that he might be able to get some useful information.

Having been raised in Eastern Kentucky, Avery knew a little bit about things like edible plants and wild mushrooms, but he didn't know nearly enough. He found himself driving to the building and pulling into the parking lot, patting Tilly on the head as he cut the engine.

"Just give me a couple of minutes. I think I can find what I'm looking for pretty quick," he told her, and the beagle just laid down in the seat with a hefty sigh as she realized she wasn't joining him inside.

The elevators were obviously useless now, so Avery took the stairs two at a time up to the top floor. He was sweating and breathing a bit heavy once he arrived, but he at least had the solace of knowing it would be much easier going back down. Pushing open the heavy door he sucked in another deep breath, the musty scent of books and dust tickling his nose. He sneezed a couple of times, the sound echoing through the large open room. It wasn't a huge library, not by any stretch of the imagination, but it was sufficient enough and had been quite popular in the time before Ruger.

Glancing around, Avery found the non-fiction section and then a subsection that had books about flora, fauna, and wildlife. He located a few books that looked like they could provide the information he was searching for, loading his arms up. There were books about wild berries and plants that you could use for cooking, and another about all different types of mushrooms. There were tomes about how to maintain a garden, which he figured he could use come spring if he could find seeds, and another about nuts and roots that seemed suitable. He snagged one about animal tracks and another about camping off the grid, being careful to balance them so he wouldn't drop any.

On his way back through the room, he grabbed a couple of novels for entertainment purposes, and then saw himself out. He went back down the stairs much more carefully than he had gone up, feeling each step down so he didn't trip and fall. Finally, he made it back and tipped his loot into the passenger side floorboard, beaming at Tilly as he started up the engine again.

"Alright, girl. Let's go home!"

FIVE

AVERY MADE IT BACK TO THE POST OFFICE WITH about thirty minutes to spare before dark, carrying everything inside before grabbing a bucket from a stack in the corner. He headed back out and walked down by the bridge to an area where the creek was more easily accessible. He eased his way down the bank carefully, not wanting to fall in and end up freezing cold with no good way to dry out his clothes.

Once he had made it down, he dipped the bucket into the rusty-looking water and scooped up enough to boil for dinner and for cleaning purposes, trying not to slosh or spill as he climbed out again. By the time he made it back, darkness was officially creeping in, the shadows long and the sun having dipped beneath the edge of the world. He felt a sudden and immense sadness then, pausing outside the back door of the office to catch his breath and calm himself down.

Sometimes it just hit him like that, how utterly alone he really was in the world. When he was busy with things, he didn't have a lot of time to consider it, but when it was quiet, and everything was as taken care of as it could be, it was overwhelming. He would never see his family again, or any of his annoying but loveable neighbors. It was a bitter pill to swallow, which was why he very much liked assigning himself tasks and setting out to do things that were often very time consuming.

If all your time was used up, then you had none left over to dwell on. The minutes and hours were already gone, and if he was lucky, he'd be so dog-tired by bedtime that he and Tilly both passed out without much fanfare. Some nights it wasn't like that, that's what the sleeping meds were for, but he worked hard to wear himself out, which was much preferable to the alternative.

Setting the bucket down, he fetched one of the many books of matches and got a fire going in the fire pit he had taken from the neighbors. He at least had an abundance of wood, which would be nice when the weather was foul, and if need be, he could always get more. That was a small comfort, pouring some of the water into a sauce pan and the rest into a shallow pot. He put both over the fire and then headed back inside, picking over his food options.

In the end, he chose a can of condensed chicken soup, waiting for the water to boil for a bit before he added the contents of the can to it. He stirred until it was warmed through, and then he took both pots off the fire, letting them cool a bit in the chilly air. It was nice by the fire though and he elected to stay there, teetering on a milk crate that was doubling as a makeshift seat. He had a spoon and some stale saltine crackers that he dunked in the soup, eating half the pot before pouring the rest into a container with a lid. He could store it in the office lobby, which stayed frigidly cold because it was sealed off from the back area. Then tomorrow he would have breakfast, and there would be no waste.

Tilly lay beside him on a pile of dried leaves, chewing on a rawhide he'd found for her at the grocery store. She would eat her own dinner when they went inside, where wild animals and other critters wouldn't bother her or try to take her food. They had to be cautious about that sort of thing as much as they had to be careful about Avery's health. If the beagle were to tangle with some irate critter she could get badly hurt, or even sick from a bite, and there was nobody to patch her up. Avery knew enough to clean and bandage a wound, but anything beyond that would likely result in a very unfavorable ending that neither of them would want. So, really, it was better to just try and avoid the situation altogether.

That was another reason why he didn't like being out after dark either. During daylight hours he saw a few critters now and then, mostly deer and squirrels and birds, but at night other things began to prowl. There were raccoons and possums, which weren't too bad, but then there were bigger animals too. Coyotes and bobcats most noticeably, and they were likely to be growing bolder now that there weren't any humans around to cause them problems or chase them away. He wasn't ruling out the very real possibility that one or more could try to attack if he was out puttering around in the dark, so he didn't do that either.

Playing it safe was the name of the game these days, that was for sure. It was all about survival, and that also meant thinking of things you would never have thought of before. Like packs of coyotes, rabid raccoons, and other bizarre things that didn't normally cross a person's mind.

The fire was starting to fizzle out, so Avery took his leftover soup and the second pot of warm water inside. He made sure the fire was out and then called Tilly, filling up her food bowl after locking the door. Turning on a small kerosene lamp, he stored his leftovers and made sure the front door was still locked up, and then he went a step further by locking the door between the lobby and the main part of the office. It gave him peace of mind at night if nothing else.

It was chilly inside, but he wasn't ready to risk using any of his heating resources just yet, settling instead for a second sweater and sliding under the pile of blankets on his bed in the corner. He pulled out a book and tried to relax, but that didn't seem to be working tonight. He gave up after just a couple of pages, turning off the lamp to save the oil and staring up instead at the dark ceiling. He felt Tilly climb onto the mattress, and he lifted the blankets for her to get underneath, her warmth making the chill he was feeling much more tolerable.

"We've got to have a plan, Tilly," he whispered to the dog, pulling the blankets up under his chin to try and keep the cold out. "We can't stay here forever, just barely getting by. We're going to have to figure out where to go and how to get there, even if it takes most of next summer. We need to be some place warm, where it's easier to get by. A place where we won't have to worry about heat or stocking up for winter weather. It's going to be hard to leave here, but I think it has to be done. I don't think we can keep living here indefinitely, you know?"

The beagle, of course, didn't answer him, but that was okay with Avery. It just felt nice to talk a little, to use his voice even if there would never be a response. At least she was a good listener, and she certainly didn't judge him when he went on these rants.

This idea had occurred to him long before now, of course. In fact, it was something he had been considering since September when the leaves had started to turn on the trees. Anywhere he went there would be drawbacks, but there were also perks of leaving here and seeking somewhere that was warmer and where true winter wasn't a concern. Going further south was the very obvious answer, but there was just so much to consider. Transportation was the biggest problem he was facing, though he could probably get enough gas to go for quite a way before it would become a concern again. That was, of course, if the roads would be passable and that was something he wasn't sure of. He hadn't ventured too far away, only going out to the interstate once to survey the situation. From the on ramp, he had seen vehicles dotting the roadside here and there, with one or two parked in the road itself. This was a small town though, and he knew that any big cities he came across would pose bigger problems.

Quite simply he wasn't going to know anything until he just finally did it. Until the moment he got into the car and took off, he would be in the dark. That made the whole thing even scarier and it made him even more unsure about the prospect of it all. What if they left and things were worse? Or they got stuck somewhere where they couldn't get supplies or things that they would need? A vehicle could only hold so much in the way of supplies, especially a car, and upgrading to something larger would mean more gas.

"I never flew anywhere before Ruger hit," he mused out loud into the darkness, breaking the otherwise empty silence. "Never took a train either. I barely even left Graven, and now I guess I'll never do any of those things. Never fly in an airplane, never take the train somewhere to see what there is to see. I mean, I guess if we leave here, I'll see some things along the way, but it won't be the same as it would have been before. It would have been fun then, going with the whole family. Maybe driving to Disney World, or maybe somewhere out west to see the Grand Canyon or something. That would have been a real good time, but this won't be nearly that good. Probably be scary though, and I've had about enough of being scared."

Rolling over on his side, Avery felt Tilly sigh and then shift when he shifted. He pulled the pillow closer under his head and then the cover up over it, his warm breath bouncing back into his face and warming his cold nose. There were so many places, from the Carolina's all the way to Georgia and Florida, and they all sounded possible. He mulled it over in his mind, trying to picture the best place to thrive, and then his mind landed on the most solid place he could think of.

"Maybe Louisiana," he muttered sleepily, his tired mind latching onto that and holding tight. "They get hurricanes and tropical storms down there, but we could hold out through one of those. Why couldn't we? We've made it through this; a hurricane isn't anything."

Avery didn't know if that were exactly true or not, he'd never been through anything worse than a strong thunderstorm, but he liked giving himself something to believe in. Louisiana would definitely be warm, and he knew from books and television that it was a swampy place with good fishing and probably good hunting too. He wasn't skilled at that yet, but he was willing to learn and try his best if it meant keeping himself and his dog fed and alive. They could move into some big old plantation house, take over all the rooms, sleep in a different bed every night of the week, and cook meals outside all year long.

He fell asleep with that lodged in his brain, thinking about antebellum homes with tall columns on the wrap around porches. He dreamed about cooking beans in a big pot outside and running barefoot in December. He dreamed about Jessa, his little sister, in one of those old-fashioned dresses with the big hoops underneath, running wild around the house with Tilly chasing along behind her. He dreamed of his mother, smiling from the back steps, and his father watching from the comfort of his rocking chair that creaked slowly back and forth.

Even in sleep, tears filled Avery's eyes, like his subconscious knew that it would never be that way. Anywhere he went from now on, he would be going alone, just him and Tilly against the empty world.

SIX

October 2017

THEY HADN'T GONE TO TOWN FOR DAYS, LIVING off the food they had stockpiled in the kitchen cabinets and in the cellar underneath the house. There were still a few things left in the garden, mostly cucumbers that were hanging on to the bitter end, but almost everything had already been picked and canned at the end of the summer. Avery's mother, Jemma, was insistent that they could live off what they had for a few months and that by that point, things would be over and done with. Every day, there were updates on the television news about vaccinations and possible remedies. Doctors around the world worked overtime to try and find a proper cure. So far, there had been no luck, however, and more and more people were succumbing to the Ruger virus every single day.

There had been few deaths reported so far in their area, and not enough people were taking the situation as seriously as they should have been. It drove Jemma Harris mad that folks were ignoring the warnings and going about their usual business, but all she could do was make sure her own family was being as careful as they could be and taking all the necessary precautions recommended by the CDC.

In the end, it wouldn't be enough. Nothing would ever prove effective against Ruger, not even isolation or quarantine, and the people of Graven, Kentucky, and the surrounding area found out the hard way. It started with the young ones, a little kid a few miles down the road coming down with a fever and dying in just a couple of days. The boy had been just four, and he was closely followed into sickness by his older brother and then a cousin. It hit the elderly next, spreading like wildfire through a local nursing home and rehabilitation facility. Six deaths in, most of the nurses and essential staff fled the area, leaving only a handful of people behind to help care for those who were left alive inside. It took two weeks for the entire place to be wiped clean by death, local health officials showing up to burn the building to the ground.

It was a Tuesday morning when Jessa, Avery's nine-year-old little sister, started to cough. They were outside together, drawing water from the well, something his mother had recently started to insist upon. The water from the tap came out in fits now, and sometimes it was murky colored and cloudy. The water from their well was clear and cool, drawn up from a deep underground spring that fed all the wells in their little neighborhood. He had just pulled up the bucket and was carefully emptying the contents into an empty milk jug to carry back to the house when Jessa was overcome, leaning forward as she heaved and hacked. She was coughing so hard she started to gag, looking pale when she finally was able to stand upright.

"You okay?" Avery asked, giving her a long look-over. Her skin was a bit sallow-looking and she was dark beneath her eyes, like someone who hadn't slept in days. She had said nothing about feeling bad the night before over breakfast, but she certainly looked unwell now. "We should get this water back to the house; a cool drink might help."

Despite being October, it was still warm, so much so that they weren't wearing jackets or even long sleeves to do their outside chores. The sun was high overhead, but it wasn't too hot, just the right kind of weather to feel comfortable all around. Jessa looked decidedly *un*comfortable though as they trekked back to the house, dragging her feet and moving slowly. She had another fit of coughing on the front porch and this drew their mother outside, touching Jessa's forehead with the back of her wrist.

Jemma reacted fast, gathering her daughter up in her arms and hurrying into the house. She was barking out orders as she went, already heading upstairs. "Avery, get the thermometer out of the medicine cabinet! Bring it up here with a glass of cold water and a cool cloth and be quick about it!"

Avery put one jug in the fridge and poured a glass of water from the second before using some of what was left to wet a cloth. He got the thermometer and then followed his mother upstairs, where she now had Jessa resting in her bed. She looked sort of sweaty now, not protesting as their mother put the thermometer beneath her tongue. It was digital, so it was just a matter of waiting for the beep to sound, and when it did Jemma Harris made a soft noise of despair.

"She's running a fever," she whispered aloud to Avery, glancing at him before taking the water and the cold cloth. "Get out of here, son. Your sister is sick; I don't want you to risk catching it too. You and your father stay downstairs and don't come up here again unless I call for you, do you understand? You've already been exposed, and that's bad enough. Go on!"

Avery started to protest, especially when he saw the scared look on Jessa's face, but he did as he was told. He slipped out of the room and shut the door behind him, moving back downstairs in a sort of daze. They had been so careful, following all the rules set by the CDC. They weren't making unnecessary trips out in public, they were washing all their food before they ate it, and they were staying away from the sick or potentially sick. Plenty of kids that Jessa had gone to school with had already fallen ill. Some were already dead, but they hadn't seen those kids in well over a month since the virus had first started to spread. What had happened?

He was still pondering on it when their father returned over an hour later, having gone up into the woods to try and find some wild game for them to fill their winter freezer with. It was another recommendation from the center for disease control that people avoid buying anything farm raised, still operating under the assumption that the Ruger virus could have spread from pigs to people through dirty conditions. It was possible that meats from such places could be tainted. So they had been extra safe and had thrown out what meat they had in the freezer and had stuck to wild animals if and when they felt like they needed more protein.

Telford Harris was empty handed and looking rather unhappy about it as he climbed onto the back porch, Avery meeting him before he could even get up the steps. He was surprised to see his son there in front of him, though the look on the boy's face put him on high alert. "What is it? What's wrong?" He asked, already shedding his boots as he started toward the back door.

"It's Jessa," Avery answered, trailing close behind him. "She's sick, dad. Got a cough and a fever and all that. Mom is up there with her but said we're supposed to stay down here. She doesn't want to risk exposing us to anything. It might not be Ruger though, right? It might just be a cold or a regular infection or something couldn't it? I mean, we all got sick with stuff before this started going around; people can still get regular sick."

"She has a fever?" Telford asked, as though clarifying what he had just heard. He dropped his boots by the door and looked up at the ceiling, as though it would somehow give him answers as to what was going on upstairs. All they heard was the soft shuffling of feet and then nothing again, the house eerily quiet. "Did she say how high? When did this start?"

Avery felt a bit like he was talking in circles, but he knew that his father was just worried and so he obliged him without any sort of complaint. It was easier to just get on with telling it and answering the questions despite already having given the answers. "Just a little over an hour ago. She seemed alright, and then we went to get water and she started to cough. How could this happen, dad? If she does have it, then how did she get it? None of our neighbors are sick yet, and we've not been around anybody but each other."

His father was quiet for a long time, pulling out a chair at their small kitchen table and dropping into it heavily. Telford's head stayed tilted back toward the ceiling though his eyes were closed, something he did when he was really thinking about something. After a little while he got out of the chair and went to the fridge, pulling out the full jug of well water. He sat it down on the counter and just stared at it, Avery watching him curiously.

"Water," he said finally, looking over at his son with his mouth set into a frown. "We stopped drinking the tap water because it looked rough, right? Like maybe there aren't enough people anymore working at the plant, and like maybe they aren't doing the job well anymore. We thought it was dirty water, tainted water, so we started using the well water. The thing is, we aren't the only family here that gets water from the same spring; a whole bunch of us do. Lots of people with lots of different sanitation habits all dipping into the same pool. We don't know what is in this water, or even really where the source is starting from. There are lots of folks saying this could be spreading through water, and maybe they ain't wrong. Maybe they're very, very right."

Avery's eyes got big then, having never considered that as even a remote possibility. Could disease spread through water? He knew enough to know that some things could and that they did, but nobody knew all that much about Ruger yet. He'd not heard anything on the television about water testing, at least nothing that was serious or scientific, so the possibility of it felt very much real now.

"What do we do, though? We have to drink *something*," he brought up finally, biting his lower lip as he looked at his dad with worry on his face.

"We boil the water from here on out, no matter where it's come from. Even if it's the bottled stuff in the cellar, just to be cautious. It may be too late now, no way of knowing that, but we gotta do better if we're gonna survive," Telford answered his son, getting a pot from under the stove. He put it on a burner and emptied the jug of water into it, cranking the heat up on high to get it to boiling. "Once it's done, let it cool off, and then put it in a new container. Throw out the ones we've already used, alright? They might be contaminated."

"Yes, sir," Avery answered quickly, knowing it was something he needed to do, and he was glad for it because it would give him a small focus.

His father headed for the stairs then, looking weary as he started up them. Avery started to remind him of his mother's orders but thought the better of it. Telford knew what Jemma had said for them to do, and he'd made up his mind to disregard her at least somewhat. So, Avery settled for listening instead, his father disappearing at the top of the landing. He followed his heavy footsteps that seemed to stop somewhere near Jessa's room, and then he heard a deep but muffled voice. Moments later he was answered by a voice a little further away, meaning that his parents were communicating through Jessa's still closed bedroom door.

The water boiled, and Avery kept it on the burner for a while just to play it safe. He then set it aside to let it cool, throwing out the used jugs and getting out a new one that had previously held juice. He used a bit of the now sterilized water to rinse it out and then filled it with the rest, screwing the lid on and putting it back into the fridge. His father was still upstairs, so he put away his boots and the gun he'd left propped up on the back porch, venturing out to make sure the cover was on the well. The water might have been tainted, but they also didn't want a coon or a squirrel falling into it and drowning. That would create a whole host of other problems, that much he knew for certain.

Back inside, Avery opened a can of soup and got it steaming for his dinner, filling a bowl and drifting into the living room. He put the news on, which was just about the only thing even on these days and listened to all the latest updates of which there were few. None of them had much to say either, at least nothing beneficial, and he ended up finishing dinner with a rerun episode of The Office, which didn't even make him crack a smile.

He had laid down across the sofa and fallen asleep by the time his father came back down, wearing clean sweatpants and a t-shirt. He took the rest of the soup and ate it cold from the pot while he sat in his recliner, not speaking until well after the pot was empty, and sat down on the coffee table.

"Her fever has gotten worse," Telford told Avery, watching a news alert flash across the bottom of the screen. Someone in the government had died, some senator, and it was as though it was finally dawning on people that power and money couldn't save you. "Spiked higher, and she's sweating more. Your mother…your mother doesn't think this is just a run of the mill infection, Avery, or a common cold. She's really hot, so hot she's bordering on delirious. We talked a bit about sending you out to the ridge to your grandmother's house, but we've decided that you need to stay here with us. It's not fair to you or to your grandmother, because you've already been exposed. So, we just have to sit tight and wait this out, okay? Let's just pray we're wrong and that Jessa gets better in the night."

Jessa did not, in fact, improve. She got worse overnight, shivering for hours and then sweating and tossing and turning. It was as though her body was at war with itself, unable to make a decision on how it should react to whatever it was that was going on. It was around six a.m. when she started throwing up, Jemma racing into the bathroom for the mop bucket so she had something to vomit into. Avery and Telford listened to it all from the living room they had been sequestered to, unable to help and unsure about what else to do.

A few hours later, Jemma did call down asking for more water and some crackers, and Avery took them up to her. He put them outside the bedroom door along with some children's Tylenol, another cool cloth, and a sandwich for his mother. He said a few things to his sister through the door too, letting her know that he loved her and that she was going to get better soon. There was no answer from Jessa, only the quiet sound of his mother suppressing a sob.

They lived in this strange state of flux for three days, with Avery and Telford delivering things upstairs to Jessa's bedroom door, mother and daughter locked away inside with a towel stuffed under the crack between the door and the floor. They did leave the bedroom window open whenever Jessa's fever ramped up, trying to keep down the sweats and make her more comfortable. Avery saw the curtain flapping in the breeze whenever he went to fetch more water to boil, hoping to catch a glimpse of his mother and sister inside. He never did though, he only saw that bright floral print pattern rippling against the wind.

On the morning of the third day Jemma finally left her daughter's bedroom, disappearing into the bathroom that Avery had once shared with Jessa. They heard the water running, but neither of them had the heart to go up and tell her their theory on tainted water. Instead, they just continued to listen from below as she got into the tub and thumped around for about an hour until the water finally drained out. They followed her footsteps to the master bedroom, doors opening and closing several times. Finally, Jemma descended the staircase, wearing clean clothes and looking distraught.

"She's gone," she whispered before collapsing into her husband's arms, Telford catching her before she could hit the floor. Avery watched at his parents held one another and sobbed uncontrollably, though he felt unable to do so himself. It made him feel guilty that he had no tears, but he couldn't make them come.

What he felt was angry, a rage building up inside of him against everyone and everything. Why hadn't the doctors and scientists done more? Why hadn't they figured this out already? What was the point of living in a world where you carried all the answers in the universe in your pocket in the form of a phone if they couldn't keep little girls from dying of a stupid fever? He wanted to scream, to yell, to break things but instead, he went upstairs and into the bathroom.

He found rubber gloves beneath the sink and he gathered up the clothes his mother had discarded, stuffing them all into a bag. He carried them outside and put them into the burn barrel where they disposed of their garbage, tossing the gloves in too. He went back into the house and tidied up the kitchen and then got on the phone, calling the number that they had been instructed to dial if someone in their home fell victim to Ruger.

"I called the emergency services number," he announced when he finally got back into the living room, his father cradling his mother against his side on the sofa now. "They said they'd be here within the hour, and they're coming from King's Daughters hospital. I didn't think you'd be up to calling, so I went ahead and did it."

Avery had heard stories about the emergency services line that had been put into play after Ruger began to spread. They came to your house and collected the bodies of your loved ones, disposing of them in a way that was supposed to prevent further spread of the disease. That was all he really knew about it since they didn't talk too much about it on television. Speaking about body removal and disposal made it too real somehow, less like something to talk about and something that had to be dealt with, but they had reached that point and that meant they had no other choices left.

"Oh, Avery," Jemma whispered, shaking her head at him. Both parents were just staring as though he had done something awful, and he couldn't imagine how this had been the wrong thing. "They'll take her away from us! She deserves to be buried, to be put to rest in a proper way. Who knows what they'll do with her!"

"You're the one who told me that this has to be taken seriously," Avery pointed out, anger rushing through him all over again. How could she really be mad at him for doing the things he had been impressing upon him since the whole thing had started? "If we bury her, it might spread somehow, unless you somehow do it in a way that means nobody can ever come in contact with her even after she's dead. We have to do it the safe way, the best way, because that's the only way there is now. I loved Jessa too; I didn't want this to happen to her, but it did, and this is what they said to do."

Jemma started crying all over again, Telford wrapping his arms around her without so much as glancing at his son. Avery knew they were distraught, that they wouldn't hate him forever, but for the moment, he felt like a puppy who had piddled on the rug. He left the house and went out through the front, situating himself on the steps to wait for the people who were coming to take Jessa to show up.

They did and right on schedule too, almost exactly one hour after he had put in the call. They came in a white van with a medical insignia on the side, two men and a woman exiting the vehicle. They all wore outfits that looked quite a lot like hazmat suits, complete with masks that made them breathe like Darth Vader. Two of them entered the house while the third gathered materials out of the back, approaching Avery slowly.

"You live here?" The woman asked, an echo to her voice as it came out sounding filtered from the mask.

Avery nodded his head slowly, wanting to ask a million questions but operating under the assumption that this lady probably didn't really feel like having to answer them. "Yeah, I do. My little sister just died."

The woman was sorting through the items she'd brought from the van, finally pulling out a sign that had a biohazard symbol on it. "I'm sorry to hear that. Were you all exposed to her while she had the fever?"

"Me and my mom were, yeah, but my dad was out hunting. He was never around her after she started to get sick," he told her carefully, trying to work out why they were asking. The lady put the sign up on their door, and beneath with a black sharpie wrote the number three very carefully. "Hey, what's that for? Why are you putting that sign on our door?"

"Because you're all potentially infected, and it means you're capable of spreading the virus. You'll be quarantined inside of your home for two weeks, which is how long it can take for some people to show the signs and symptoms of the Ruger virus. This sign means that this house has experienced infection and that someone inside is either currently ill or has recently passed away. There are currently three of you who live here that have been exposed, so we're able to keep track of how many people there are at any given time that are possible carriers. We do this to every house we visit, it isn't just yours."

Avery felt his mouth drop open a little, panic rising a bit in his chest. Quarantined? What exactly did that mean in this situation? They hadn't mentioned any of this on the phone, and he suddenly wished he hadn't done the supposed right thing. His mother may just have been right in a way, and while he didn't think that burying Jessa was the safest route, perhaps calling these people hadn't been the best idea either.

"So, what? We can't leave our house?" He asked, watching as she got out a big roll of tape and laid it aside. "We have to be able to go outside! Our tap water is horrible, we're drinking well water, and the well is away from the house. We can't just be locked up in here!"

"We'll give you a kit that contains things you'll need during the quarantine process. We have water filtration tablets for those experiencing poorly filtered drinking water, as well as some medical supplies including masks and gloves. Don't worry; if none of you show any symptoms within two weeks, then we'll clear the home, and you'll be free to go," she told him with a nod. "I suggest you all take the time you're inside to clean everything. Use bleach if you have it, and get rid of anything that Jessa had close contact with during the fever. Burn it in a fireplace or something if you have it; fire is the best way."

Fire is the best way. Avery's stomach turned again, as he had a pretty good idea now of how they planned to dispose of Jessa's body. He felt like he might throw up, but he knew that could be a death sentence in front of these people, so he swallowed it down. Instead, he just nodded a little, hearing a bit of commotion as the two men came through the door. They were carrying Jessa inside of a zipped-up black bag, his mother stumbling behind them. The woman caught her though and nudged her back inside, nodding for Avery to join his parents in the front hall.

"I'm sure the others briefed you, but I want to do a quick refresher. Two weeks is how long we expect you to stay inside, and we will be checking in. Once this door is shut we'll be putting tape over the door frames and along with all the windows. If that tape is broken or tampered with in any way, then we know you left or at least attempted to leave the home. We can't have that. Our job is to help prevent the spread of this disease, and I know that you all understand just how serious this can be. I don't want to have to deal with any problems and given what you've just been through, I don't think you do either," she told them, looking at them each in turn through the little plastic window in her mask. "Two weeks, Harris family, that's all we're asking for. Your compliance is paramount."

With that, she reached in and shut the door on them. For the next twenty minutes they listened as the people moved around their house, peeling long strips of heavy tape to put over the doors and windows. Eventually, they left with Jessa in tow, leaving behind the three remaining members of the family.

"You should never have called," Telford whispered, voice a little bit shaky as he moved from window to window, as though he were trying to call their bluff. "Now we're trapped in here like mice in a cage, just waiting to get sick and die."

"Don't blame Avery," Jemma answered, wiping carefully at her teary eyes. "He was just doing what he thought was best, and I can't fault him for that. I'm sorry that I got upset before, I know why you did it honey." She paused and then let out a very heavy sigh. "Come on. Let's get trash bags and bleach and clean out Jessa's room as best we can. We can use the fireplace to burn things, and once the quarantine is up, we can get rid of the bigger things like the mattress. They left us a kit; we can use the gloves and masks that are inside."

Avery finally noticed the big box sitting on the living room coffee table. That same medical looking insignia was on the side. He hadn't bothered to ask what it meant or really who had even sent them, and it was too late to care now. Instead he just did as his mother requested and opened it up, finding heavy gloves and surgical masks inside. She got the bleach, a clean bucket to throw their refuse in, and some old rags to scrub with.

They left Telford pacing downstairs as they headed up together, going single file into Jessa's empty bedroom. The first thing that hit Avery was the smell, which was pungent even with the mask on it. It smelled sour, like old milk almost, and his mother told him it was the bucket that she'd put under the table by the bed. He bagged that up first, careful not to look at the contents, and sat it in the bathtub where he shut the door. The next thing he noticed was the blood speckling her floral print bed sheets, like someone had misted red all over everything.

"I'm sorry that this happened," Avery told his mother gently as he began to strip the sheets off, his heart pounding in a way that made him feel a bit dizzy. "I'm sorry too that I called those people. I thought I was helping, not making things worse."

Jemma helped him stuff the sheets and blankets into a large trash bag, just nodding at him a little as she tied it closed. "I know you were, and I'm not angry anymore. I know that they're trying to keep other people from getting sick, and I respect that you wanted to do the same. I'm also glad that you listened to the things I was telling you, and that you were able to keep a calm head even though I wasn't."

Avery stuffed Jessa's pillows into another bag, putting everything into the corner to be collected and taken to the fireplace downstairs. When he bent over to grab her slippers though he saw something on the floor between her bed and night table, reaching out to grab it. It was her stuffed pig, Orville, that she had had since she was a baby. She had slept with Orville religiously, and now here he was trapped near the floor and spotted with Jessa's blood.

That was when he finally lost it, the tears coming hot and fast. He slid down to sit on the floor with Orville still in his gloved hands, sobbing so hard he started to choke. He felt his mother's arms around him then, hugging him hard and tight against her. She told him to let it out, that it was okay, even though he knew it really wasn't. They had been so careful, had tried so hard, and they had still lost Jessa. None of them were safe, they would never be safe again, and now they really did have to play an awful waiting game. Would they live? Would they get sick? Even if they didn't get sick in the next two weeks, they probably would eventually.

What was the point? What were they even doing anymore?

He cried until he couldn't cry anymore, his mother taking Orville away and putting him into a fresh bag. Eventually he got up off the floor, and they continued dousing everything they couldn't burn right away in bleach, including the mattress. They took the bags downstairs and started a fire, tossing things in one at a time until it was all gone. Her room was shut up again, and they bleached the bathroom too, though they all agreed to use the one downstairs just to be safe.

Once that was done, everything as sanitized as it could be, they settled in for the longest and saddest two weeks of their lives.

SEVEN

November 2017

THE FINAL DATE OF THE FAMILY QUARANTINE came and went, and the emergency medical response team returned to the house to free them. It was a bewildering thing, suddenly being free after two weeks of lockdown, but nothing much seemed to change even after the signs and tape came down, and the team left them alone again. Avery continued bringing in water from the well, a nice change after drinking double-boiled tap water that they still had to drop the tablets into. It left the water tasting funny, metallic, and unpleasant, and so boiled well water was a great alternative.

Jemma Harris busied herself with inventorying what food and other things they had in the house and down in the cellar, which she had instructed her husband to help secure. Telford reinforced the cellar doors with a few metal bars, adding a heavy chain and a thick padlock. They weren't worried about running out of food any time soon, there was plenty for just the three of them, but looting was a very real concern. Every day on the news, they saw stories of people becoming more and more desperate and aggressive, doing everything they could to assure that their own families could get by. It wasn't worth the risk, and though they wanted to trust their neighbors it felt better to just take precautions.

The weather grew increasingly gloomy and cool, October slipping by with each day very much similar to the last. They still planned meals twice a day, a snack between them, and the constant need to draw water, boil it clean, and store it away for future use. They had used up every container in the house it seemed. Jemma was obsessing over the idea of possibly running out. They did have bottled water, stored away still wrapped in plastic down in the cellar, but that was being saved for later. It was an emergency supply that went untouched despite the fact that they were, more or less, already in the midst of an emergency. Telford and Avery knew better than to argue, however, and so nobody touched a single bottle.

The idea of Thanksgiving seemed utterly ludicrous, but as the first of November came, Jemma brought it up anyway. They had things to celebrate. After all, the three of them had so far avoided illness, a true miracle considering that the Ruger virus had claimed Jessa right here in the house. The three of them were gathered in the living room around the television, watching a broadcast from Atlanta where a riot had broken out. People had marched on the CDC demanding answers, a cure, anything to bring some solace to what was going on around the globe. It had quickly escalated to violence, and now there were fires and buildings being broken into, and in one scene a group of angry people were flipping over a police car.

Avery could very much understand their rage because he was angry too. The top scientists in the world had come up short, unable to reach any conclusions or find any real answers. They were still squabbling about how the whole thing had started and where it had even come from, no closer to answers now than they had been when the whole thing had first started. It was frustrating for everyone, and for some, that frustration had grown into something greater.

As they watched, his mother brought up the idea of dinner, if his father was up to the possibility of trying to get them a wild turkey from the woods. There wasn't a whole lot to celebrate, sure, but there was enough to be thankful for, and it would be a little slice of normal in an otherwise disintegrating world. The idea was appealing, even if it was sort of silly, and Avery was asking her about mashed potatoes when they heard shouting and then car doors slamming.

Muting the television, the three of them wandered to the windows, peering out at the neighbors. They were hastily loading up their old pickup truck, tossing things into the back. Their dog, a big lab named Duke, was sitting in the cab already and panting as his owners loaded a portable Coleman grill and two coolers by lifting them over the closed tailgate.

Pushing open the front door, Telford stepped out onto the porch for a better look though he got no closer than that. "Everything alright?" He called out, prompting Mark Smalls to stop what he was doing though his wife, Margie, kept right on going.

"N'aw, we're getting out of here," Mark told him, slapping his hand against the tailgate. "Margie's mom and Jamie have done come down sick, we ain't staying here and risking it. People are saying it's not so bad out west, less people and all that, so we're going to head that way. A whole bunch of folks is goin' from town too, we're joining up in a caravan. Too many people here are sick now; it's spreading. Not a single house in these parts ain't got somebody sick or already dead. No sense in waiting anymore."

"You're leaving Nellie and Jamie behind?" Telford asked, Avery's eyes going wide as him and his mother listened. Jamie was the Smalls' six-year-old son, hardly capable of taking care of himself or his elderly grandmother. "You can't leave them alone over there, Mark! The boy will be scared enough as it is; he needs his parents there with him!"

Avery had a good idea that his father was thinking about Jessa and about how Jemma had stayed with her locked in that bedroom until the bitter end. It wasn't something that any parent wanted to see, but it wasn't something that a person with good morals could just turn their back on. Jamie was their child, and Nellie was Margie's mother. It was barbaric to just up and leave them to die without anyone there to give them so much as a sip of cool water on their way out.

Mark just shrugged at Telford and fished the keys out of his pocket as Margie exited the house, leaving the door standing open behind her. "We have to go, Telford, and that's just all there is to it. They're sick and there ain't nothing to do for them now. What's done is done, and I hate that it has to be this way, but it does. We called that number, the same one you all called when Jessa passed, they're on their way. We wanna be long gone by then, sure as hell don't want to risk getting locked up in there with two sick ones like ya'll did. Take care, now. I suggest you all get out while you can too, before time has done run out."

Avery and his mother drifted to the porch then too, standing behind Telford and just watching as half of the Smalls family climbed into the truck with their dog and left. They stayed there watching as the emergency team returned, different people this time around though, and headed into the house. They were there for what felt like a small eternity, but when they did exit it was with Nellie, who had to be carried by two men and was strapped down to a backboard, and little Jamie who was holding the hand of one of the team members and wearing a mask. They were loaded into the van, and then one of the people went back, locking the front door and closing it up, putting a sign on the door before they drove away.

It had started to grow dark by then, and up and down the road, there were fewer lights than there had ever been before. For the first time, Avery noticed that several other houses bore similar signs, and all of those homes were dark. A few more had no cars in the driveway anymore, people that had likely flown the coop out west just like the Smalls were doing now.

"It's stupid," Avery said out loud then, wrapping his arms around himself as a cool wind whipped around them. "Going out west, I mean, it's stupid. People out west are getting sick just the same as people here are. We don't live in a place with a lot of people, and it's still spreading. Anywhere you go, it's going to follow; there's no way to get away from it. People can riot all they want or leave home, but it's all just pointless. They should have stayed with

Jamie, because it's just not going to matter either way."

Jemma put her arm around Avery's shoulders and led him back inside, leaving Telford behind on the porch. He was still staring into the distance with a haunted look on his face and didn't join them back inside the house until over an hour later. They ended up turning the television off altogether after that and going to bed early, all of them a little bit shook by what had transpired tonight.

Avery eventually drifted off to sleep thinking about Jamie Smalls, about where they had taken him and Nellie. Had they gone to a hospital where they could be made comfortable until they died? Was there some sort of facility that none of them even knew about? He wasn't sure, and it made him restless, so that he slept in fits and starts all through the night.

The next morning dawned colder than the last, none of them hungry enough to bother making anything for breakfast. They listened to the radio that morning, more talk about Atlanta with an official statement by the CDC about their continued dedication to putting an end to the spread of the virus. It all sounded like a bunch of malarkey now, just lip service in an effort to prevent any further trouble from cropping up. Avery supposed it was probably better than just letting everyone stay riled up, but then again words were unlikely to stop most people. He was just glad they didn't leave in a big city, that things here were at least mellow and slow by comparison.

That afternoon, two more cars left from neighboring houses, loaded down with people and belongings. At that point, Telford opted to drive into town, wanting to see what was going on. He promised to stay in the truck and not to get out, heading off in the direction of the main road just after the lunch hour.

He didn't return until nearly five that evening when dinner was on the stove, and Avery had drawn in more water. He looked frazzled and tired, shedding his shoes and coat by the front door and going to scrub up for dinner in a pot of warm water. They had stopped using what came out of the tap completely, heating well water for all their everyday uses. It wasn't convenient, but it seemed more sanitary on the whole.

"Well?" Jemma finally asked as they sat down at the table, serving everyone a steaming bowl of stew since it was so cold out today. "What was going on? Did you find out anything?"

"Mark Smalls was right," Telford explained to them, dipping a piece of freshly baked bread into his stew. He chewed in silence for a moment, using his full mouth to try and get his thoughts together. "People are leaving, and not just a few either. It's like everyone is suddenly trying to get out. There were a lot of houses in town with those biohazard signs on the doors and a few that are sealed up which means there are sick people inside under quarantine. There was a lot of traffic, and there were accidents all over the place, which is what took me so long. The police have shut their doors, so there's nobody to direct traffic or any of that. Everyone is just doing what they please, and everything bottle necked around an overturned truck."

Avery tried to imagine their small town in a state of disarray like his father was describing but it was hard to do so. Nothing much ever happened, and certainly nothing to create a traffic jam like that. The population of the town was less than four thousand people, though if people came out of the woodwork from the backroads and unincorporated areas he supposed that it would cause a lot of commotion. He still couldn't picture it, though, burning his tongue on a bite of soup since he was too focused on what his dad was telling him to pay enough attention.

"Is anything in town still open?" Jemma asked then, not even having picked up her spoon yet. She was staring at Telford too, her hands resting in her lap.

Telford shook his head slowly, blowing a bit at a spoonful of soup to cool it down before he took the bite. "Most things are closed up tight; if it wasn't for the traffic, the place would be a ghost town. The hardware store and the pharmacy had boarded up their windows and doors, and the grocery store had done the same, but people had pried the plywood off the front door and broken in. I'm not sure what they were hoping to find, there couldn't have been all that much left, but I guess they got whatever was left to get."

"What will people do for medicine and food?" Avery asked then, mouth set into a frown. He knew that they were advising people to avoid crowded places or going out at all if it could be helped, but it seemed so insane to him that they would just shut everything down. This was how it was on television and in comics when the zombies invaded, and everyone ran scared. This wasn't a piece of fiction though, this was real life, and it shouldn't be possible.

"There's no need for medicine now, son," Telford answered after a moment of silence, still eating his soup as though they weren't discussing something so heavy and awful. "I guess they figure if you got something bad enough to kill you that it might be better to let it take you before the virus to gets you. Same with food, if you haven't got any stored up by now, there's really no use. It's too little too late, this thing is here, and there's no time left to prepare."

His father's answer felt so bleak and hopeless, and it left Avery with a strange hollow feeling in his gut. Eventually, he picked his spoon back up and began to eat, though Jemma announced she wasn't very hungry and gave her bowl to Telford and her bread to Avery, letting them finish it off. They heated water to wash the dishes like they did every night now, cleaning up from their meal and storing the leftover stew to have for breakfast or lunch the next day.

The cable had dwindled down to just three stations still on the air, reporting news and weather nearly around the clock. Sometimes they showed reruns if there wasn't much to report on, but tonight they were all reporting the same fire at a vaccination manufacturer in Chicago, an apparent act of terrorism meant to scare the establishment into.... something. Avery wasn't honestly sure what the purpose was, and he excused himself to head upstairs to read some before bed.

Just after midnight, he shut off his light, and tossed aside his book to the foot of his bed. His beagle, Tilly, had curled up beside him, and he threw an arm around her as he drifted off. She had been a trooper of a dog, living outside on scraps and what he could toss her from the upstairs windows during their quarantine, but she had never left. She had stayed right there at home, loyal to her person, and he was thankful for that. Tilly was one of the few good things he had left in the world, and he held onto her tighter than ever.

He was vaguely aware of someone else coming upstairs an hour or so later, the door to the master opening and then shutting again gently so as not to wake him. He stirred a little and then drifted again, the mattress squeaking as he shifted a bit to escape Tilly's hot doggy breath on his face. He turned onto his back and sprawled, one leg out from under the covers and an arm draped over his eyes. The moon shone brightly through his bedroom window, lying across the room in fat stripes of white light. He was dreaming about Thanksgiving, turkey and all the trimmings on the table, and Jessa was there. She was laughing and talking, and everything was the way it had been before, something he found himself longing desperately for.

It was a noise from downstairs that woke him up with a start, sitting bolt upright in bed as his heart began to pound in his chest. It had sounded like a sonic boom, something impossibly loud and hard to believe. It was such a quiet night, like all nights had been for weeks and months now, and that sound had shattered the nighttime silence like a brick through a window. He heard the master bedroom door fly open, creating a lesser crashing sound as it slammed into the adjacent wall.

"Telford!" He heard his mother scream his father's name, but he still wasn't putting the pieces together. He felt so impossibly tired despite the scare, and his brain hadn't fully caught up to the situation just yet. There were footsteps pounding down the stairs and then a scream, the hair rising up on the back of his neck. That got him out of bed and moving finally, Tilly ambling after him.

Avery found his mother in the living room, kneeling in front of his father's chair. The first thing he saw after his eyes fell on her was Telford's hunting rifle, which was resting on the floor beside her. The pieces began to come together now, and he put his hands over his mouth as he turned away to silence his own sudden want to scream. The noise that had shaken him from sleep had not been a sonic boom but instead the blast of a rifle coming from almost directly below his bedroom.

His vision began to fade in and out then, and he knew that he was going to pass out. He managed to lower himself to the floor before it happened, bringing up his knees and resting his forehead against them. Tilly came then and whined at him, nudging him with her wet nose. He didn't respond, he just kept sucking in deep breaths of air to try and keep himself from totally letting go.

It felt as though hours slipped by before his mother managed to get herself up, grabbing a sheet from the linen closet. She covered her husband and then came to sit beside of her son, wrapping her arms around them. They hugged each other there on the floor until the sun began to rise outside, light seeping in through the window curtains. Both knew that they would have to do something, they couldn't just stay like this, but neither was willing to be the first to move.

Finally, it was Jemma who whispered that they had to clean things up, rising to her feet again. She paced a bit, moving between the living room and the kitchen, and that was when she found the note that was held in place by a magnet on the front of the refrigerator. It was written in Telford's awkward and blocky handwriting, all the things there on paper that he hadn't been able to say to the both of them out loud. He was afraid of getting sick, of letting the virus take him the way it had taken Jessa. He didn't want to burden the pair of them with another sick person, and he was also tired of just waiting. Waiting to get sick, waiting for the fever to come, waiting to die. Watching the way things were falling apart around them, people trying to run from something they couldn't out pace, had finally gotten to him. It was better this way, he assured them, and though he loved them this was just what he felt that he had to do.

Avery listened as his mother read the letter aloud, wishing that he could commiserate with what his father was saying, but he couldn't. It felt like being abandoned, like just giving up, and it didn't sit right with him. What had happened to Jessa and to countless others was horrible, yes, but maybe things would get better soon. There was no way of knowing, no way of seeing into the future, and it just felt like tossing aside what little bit of hope there was left in the world and stomping on it.

Reading the letter felt like taking the wind out of their sails again, but they still had to deal with the situation. There were no police to come, no ambulance to be called out, so it was up to them. They kept Telford wrapped tight in the sheet, which Avery was immensely thankful for. No matter what happened or how he felt, he never wanted to see his father like that. They carried him out back and laid him on the cold ground, returning for the chair which was blood soaked and ruined. They sat the chair in a flat area near the top of the lawn, and then they sat Telford in it again. Avery found the can of gas in the shed that they kept for the mower, letting his mother carry out the task of dousing the chair and the sheet with it.

He couldn't stand to stay and watch the fire, heading into the house as his mother lit the bottom of the sheet. He heard a whooshing sort of sound, and he knew the fire had taken, eating up the soaked material quickly. Avery shivered at the sound and shut the door behind him, folding himself into a kitchen chair as he waited for his mother to come inside with him.

As he waited, he thought about Jessa, and how she had only been gone a mere few weeks. His mother had been upset when they had come to take her away, wanting to bury her instead in the family plot of the local cemetery. That hadn't even been brought up today, an option that was no longer on the table, and he felt slightly amazed. So much had changed in so little time, and it seemed to have just happened and been accepted without either of them fully realizing it. There had been no need to even discuss what would happen with Telford's body, it was just somehow common knowledge between them, something they were both aware of and seemed to understand. While Avery couldn't personally stand to participate, couldn't bring himself to be part of it, he hadn't protested either. This was just how it had to be now, this was the new normal, and that was that.

A little while later, Jemma came inside, smelling like smoke with soot smudging her pink wind nipped cheeks and her eyes red from crying. Avery had cried too, quietly at the kitchen table, but had forced himself up to heat the left-over stew. They ate in silence, not really tasting the meal, and he cleared the dishes and washed everything up while his mother took a shallow bath upstairs using cold water.

That night they didn't put the news on; they didn't even bother to migrate into the living room. Instead, they played the radio, where the music was interrupted every few minutes with pointless news breaks, and sat at the table putting together a puzzle that Avery had retrieved from the hall closet.

There were just two of them now, the last remnants of the Harris family. Down a father and a daughter, both ripped violently and suddenly from the world. It felt so wrong, but there wasn't anything they could do about it. Mother and son had to carry on, trying to make it now when the odds were very much stacked against them.

EIGHT

November 2017

A FEW DAYS AFTER AVERY'S FATHER TOOK THE SO-called easy way out, the looters came. They arrived on the cusp of a late fall storm, the smell of rain in the air and a heavy wind moving through the tree tops. He and his mother might not have noticed them as quickly if they hadn't been outside, bringing in the clothes they'd put out to dry on their make-shift clothesline. The power was an iffy thing these days, going off and on at a whim, so it wasn't exactly resourceful to rely on the dryer anymore. They still used the washer, they could always rinse the clothes by hand if it quit in the middle of a cycle, but it was easier now to just toss things onto the line they'd strung up between the front porch posts while the weather was still warm enough during the day to warrant it.

They were folding towels when they heard voices approaching, hearing them well before seeing them. Everything was so quiet these days, and even the animals had become still and silent as the storm approached. Their sound echoed through the narrow valley; high-pitched laughter flecked with coughing and the occasional whoop of delight, which sent a shiver straight down Avery's spine. What was there to laugh about so heartily these days? Nothing that he could think of, and something about it bothered him deeply. He and his mother might have been thrilled to see other people after going so many days without, but he could tell by the way her mouth was set in a deep frown that she felt like he did.

Something was wrong. Very, very wrong.

"Go inside," his mother told him then, giving him a sideways look. She was holding a pink towel in her hands, clutching it so tightly her knuckles were turning white. She was staring down the road in the direction of the voices, which were growing louder as they drew nearer. "Now, Avery!"

Avery was reluctant to leave her there alone, especially after the sound of broken glass joined the jovial sounds of the group up the road. It felt wrong to go inside while she stayed out here, and it made him feel like a coward. He also knew, however, not to question her, so he did as she told him. He stepped just inside the house, leaving the front door open so that only the screen door separated them. His heart was pounding now as he watched with her, eyes on the road as they played the waiting game.

The group moved into view, three men walking shoulder to shoulder right up the middle of the narrow country road. One of them was dragging an old grain sack along the ground, the sides bulging out at odd angles. He stopped every few feet to cough, wobbling a bit on his feet from the force of it. He was sick, that much was clear, though it was hard to tell if he had Ruger or something else. Avery didn't want to get close enough to find out, that much he knew for certain.

The others didn't exactly look much better, the two of them pale with dark circles beneath their eyes. One carried an old wooden baseball bat, which had likely been the source of the broken glass they'd heard, while the other was empty handed. They were still talking among themselves as they approached, scanning over the empty houses and abandoned buildings as they meandered. The one with the bat noticed his mother first and used the weapon to gesture towards their house, prompting all three to stop in their tracks.

"Will ya look at that! Hey, sweetheart! We sure didn't think we'd find nobody living around here! Ain't you a surprise!"

Avery bristled as the men whistled and cat-called his mother, who was standing ramrod straight with the towel still clutched in her hands. She didn't answer them, only stared back with a dark look on her face. One of the men moved closer to the steps that led up to the house from the road, but he didn't move yet to come any closer. He just gave her a wide, nasty grin that showed off a number of missing and broken teeth.

"Aw, c'mon now, sweetheart! Don't you wanna talk to us? We won't hurt ya, we promise. We just haven't seen nobody, let alone a female, in a long time," he told her, eying her up and down like she was a cut of meat at the grocery store and he was a starving man. "You alone up there, little lady?"

"No, she isn't alone!"

Avery couldn't help himself, the realization of what these men might want giving him the push to step back outside. He knew his mother might get angry with him later, but he was willing to risk that if it meant keeping her safe. "She's not alone, and you aren't welcome here. Leave."

The man with the sack began to laugh then, a little too shrill. The laughter led into another fit of coughing, and now that they were so much closer, Avery could hear the rattle in it. He could also see the flecks of blood on the man's lips, which he smeared across the back of his hand as he dragged it across his mouth. He didn't have just a common cold, that was for sure, and even though they were still all the way down on the road, Avery still took a step back.

"That's no way to treat guests," the man at the foot of the steps told Avery, taking a step up now. "We just want a little company, that's all. Why don't you go back in the house, boy? This is between us grown-ups; it's no concern to a kid like you."

"I'm not a kid, and you need to leave," Avery insisted again, reaching out to grab his mother by the wrist. "There isn't a damn thing here for you, you understand me? Not a thing."

"Oh, there's plenty for us here, I think," the man sneered, moving up another step. "More than you know. In fact, maybe we'll just stay a little while. The two of you look pretty healthy, you must have some good eats stored up in there. Hell, we won't even have to move on, we can just stay right here. Why leave when we could have everything we'd need? Of course, you might be a problem; we'll have to remedy that."

"You heard the boy; he told you to leave. I suggest you listen."

His mother finally spoke up, releasing her death grip on the pink towel. She let it fall to the floorboards of the porch, moving closer to stand shoulder to shoulder with her son. Avery could feel how rigid she was, the tension palpable now that they were so close.

He was glad though, a united front worked better than just one teenage kid making threats.

The man took one more step and then Jemma shoved Avery back into the house and followed right behind him. She slammed the door and locked it, barking at him to get the back door and to make sure they hadn't left any windows open downstairs. He was racing around checking when he heard the unmistakable sound of the shotgun barrel clicking into place, eyes wide with fear now as he hurried back to help his mother.

Jemma was standing by the front door, the loaded gun in her hands. It made Avery a little queasy to look at it, considering it was the gun his father had used just days ago, but he knew it was necessary. These men were dangerous, in more ways than one, and they couldn't risk them getting into the house. Outside he could hear them still calling out, laughing and seemingly gleeful at the knowledge that they had sent them running scared into the house. He could tell that the man on the steps hadn't made it all the way to the porch though, which was at least a small bit of relief.

Tilly joined them then, her hackles up as she came in from the kitchen. She had never liked strangers, and she certainly didn't like them so close to her house and her people. She let out an angry bay, an almost mournful sound, planting herself right beside Avery. He wondered how long the men would stay out there, taunting and tormenting, before they finally tried to get into the house. They could easily bust out windows, Avery and his mother couldn't be everywhere at once, and they could make things even more difficult by waiting for night to fall. They weren't far off from that either, as the sun set early this late in the year, so darkness would descend soon enough.

"Stay right where you are, Avery," Jemma told him then, giving him a look out of the corner of her eye. She was serious, and he knew it, so he gave her a little nod though he was loath to do it. He knelt beside Tilly on the floor and put a hand on her head, watching as his mother threw the door back open and stormed outside. "Get the hell away from my home, right now! I'm giving you to the count of ten!"

The two men on the road quieted quickly at the sight of the gun, but the one on the steps decided to call her bluff. He climbed two more steps and idly swung the bat in what was a clear move of intended intimidation. It didn't change Jemma's stance not one bit, raising the gun to aim right at the man.

"If you take one more step, you're going to regret it."

It was not a threat that Jemma was making, but a promise. She and Avery were the only remaining members of their family, and more than that they were all each other had. She would not risk these men destroying that or separating them in some way. When he moved up another step, almost the top now, she'd had enough. She pulled the trigger and fired one of the barrels, the sound of the gun blasting and the man screaming, echoing like mad through the surrounding hills.

Avery got to his feet and ran to the screen door, though he went no further as he did intend to somewhat keep his promise to his mother. He saw the man fall, though, bouncing down the old stone steps to the road like a lead weight. He hit the last step and went still, partially on his stomach with one arm trapped between his body and the road while the other stuck out at an odd angle. Blood had blossomed across the front of the ratty t-shirt he was wearing, and though he twitched and heaved for breath, he didn't try to get up.

"Do I have to fire again?" Jemma asked the remaining two men who just stood dumbfounded in the road. The one who was coughing just sat down right where he stood, while the other held his hands up and quickly shook his head. "Good. Drag him away from my steps. Now."

The man who remained standing stepped forward, afraid not to do as he was told. He grabbed hold of his buddies' feet and dragged him from the bottom of the steps to the other side of the road, right up against the low guardrail that separated the road from the creek below. He didn't seem to know what to do with himself after that, looking up at Jemma as though she would provide some sort of further guidance.

"Go," she told him, gesturing down the road with the barrel of the gun. "I don't care where, just go. And if you even think about coming back? You'll end up just like him."

The man took off then, staggering up the road without so much as a glance back. The one who had sat down was in another coughing fit and showed no signs of getting up. Avery wasn't sure if that was because he wasn't able to or what, but his mother didn't try to find out. She came back into the house, shut the door, and turned the locks. She even put on the chain, just for an extra layer of protection. Now that she was inside he could see that her hands were trembling, and he reached out to take the gun from her. He propped it up by the door and then hugged her, trying to wrap his mind around what she had just done for him. For them.

"I'm sorry you had to do that, mama," he whispered to her, his own voice carrying a slight tremble with it. "I'm so, so sorry. I should have done something about it, dad would be so upset that

I didn't."

Jemma hugged him back tightly, giving him a firm squeeze. When she pulled back, she put her hands on his face, staring at him as she spoke. "Listen to me, Avery. Nobody would be upset with you, and certainly your father wouldn't have been. It's the job of the parent to protect the child, and I would much rather go through something than you. I did what I had to do to keep you safe, and while I wish I hadn't had to…it was necessary. Sometimes the necessary things in life hurt the worst."

Letting him go, she wiped her sweaty palms on her jeans and let out a slow breath. "We stay inside the rest of the night, and we should sleep down here. That way if they try to get inside, we'll hear them sooner. We'll take care of everything else in the morning; it's getting dark soon."

The sun was low in the sky outside, and Avery knew she was right. They had plenty of water inside and leftovers from breakfast and lunch to have for dinner. So, periodically, one of them would go to the window and peer out into the darkness, searching for any figures that might be moving about. All they saw was the lump by the guardrail, and the other man who still sat in the road. They could hear him coughing, even from inside the house, and at some point, he went from sitting to laying.

Avery slept restlessly that night, and each time he woke up he'd see his mother lingering by the front door, the curtain drawn back so she could see out. By the time morning came she'd slept none, and he'd gotten only a couple of hours, which wasn't exactly restful anyway. Once he was up though, he did note he couldn't hear the cougher anymore, and a glance out showed him sprawled in the middle of the road, stiff as a board.

The pair of them busied themselves that morning, cleaning the blood off the front steps with bleach and the garden hose being the first thing they accomplished. Once that had been done they took the gas can and some matches down to the road, dousing both men in plenty of the fluid before lighting them up. They didn't stick around to watch the burning happen, neither of them could stomach it, but they kept an eye on the flames from the living room throughout the day.

They only briefly spoke about it that evening. Neither one of them was too interested in the topic but did not want to dismiss it either. They deduced that the cougher had died of Ruger, and it was very likely that his two companions had also contracted it. Perhaps Jemma had done one a favor in dispatching him so quickly, and if the third were lucky he'd have found a comfortable place to rest until the end.

After that discussion, neither of them brought it up again. They just didn't need to talk about it because it was over. It had happened, and while it did haunt them both for a while afterward, it couldn't be changed and so dwelling wasn't preferable. Eventually they shelved all those thoughts completely and put them away in the recesses of their minds.

There were, after all, more pressing things to think on.
It also turned out to be, though neither of them knew it at the moment, the last time they would ever see strangers. Or, come to that, that they would ever see anyone again except each other.

NINE

AVERY WOKE IN THE NIGHT FEELING SPOOKED, wrapped up tight in three layers of blankets with Tilly pressed against his stomach. An unfamiliar sound broke the silence that he had grown accustomed to, a mournful howling sound seeming to come from everywhere at once. It took him a moment to realize that he was hearing the wind, pushing aside the covers to crawl out into the cold night air. He shivered inside of his hooded sweatshirt and thermal underwear, getting up on his knees to push aside the blanket he'd nailed up over the window to help block the cold air.

He could see now that it was snowing hard, the wind whipping the white stuff around in the air in strange swirling patterns. His heart sank a little as he watched the storm raging out there, able to feel how cold it was when he pressed his fingertips to a pane of glass in the window. The temperature had dropped since he had crawled into bed, which was to be expected this time of year, but a snowstorm? He hadn't seen that coming at all, and he felt stupid for assuming he'd have a little bit more time before the white stuff started coming down. He could remember being a little kid and it snowing on Halloween, so this should have been a possibility in the back of his mind. The weather was an unpredictable thing these days, and he had known better than to assume and yet he had done it.

"Let's hope this blows out soon, huh?" He asked Tilly, the beagle groaning in response from beneath the covers. She was the smart one, electing to stay in their warm little nest instead of going out into the cold. He followed her back beneath the pile of blankets, taking a moment to pull on a second pair of socks.

Laying on his back with the covers drawn back up to his chin Avery just listened, the wind whistling around the back door and rattling a loose pane of glass in one of the windows. He made a mental note to tack another blanket up over the back door to help keep out any air that might seep in, not sure how much good it might do but figuring it couldn't hurt. He found himself wishing that he'd somehow found a way to insulate the place a little better, but there really wasn't anything to do about that now. Not that he knew the least little thing about building insulation anyway, so it was a silly thought no matter what.

He finally fell asleep after pulling the blanket up over his head, so his nose and ears weren't exposed to the cold. Between his body heat and the dog's, things weren't so bad, and he was able to get some good rest before morning. When he finally woke up it was still cold, though the wind seemed to have calmed down. He shimmied a pair of jeans on over his long underwear and took off a pair of socks so he could get his feet into his insulated boots. He tugged his coat on over his layers of clothes and then opened the door, greeted by a world blanketed in white.

There appeared to be several inches of snow already, and it was still falling lightly from the sky which was a steely gray color. The fire pit had to be cleaned out, but he had at least covered the wood, so it was dry and good for use. He got a fire going and was able to heat some water to wash his face and to make himself a cup of hot chocolate while he sorted out what he wanted for breakfast. He finally settled on peaches straight from the can, their syrupy sweetness almost too much for him. He didn't want to waste, so he drank the juice from the bottom and then let Tilly lick it clean, giving her a cup of dog food in her bowl.

Once they had eaten, he got a second tarp from his storage of things inside and fashioned a bit of a lean-to over the back door. He brought out a lawn chair and sat with the dog by the fire, just watching it snow. It kept it up for another hour or so before tapering off into nothing, just dull clouds, and cold.

"There is one good thing," Avery mused out loud, rubbing his hands together and holding them down over the low flames. "We won't have to go fetch water as long as there is clean snow on the ground. We can just scoop it right up and heat it, or let it melt and drink it. That won't be so bad, right? It's easier than going down into that stupid creek. This way we'll at least get to stay dry. It's definitely a more convenient situation for the moment, and convenience is not something to take for granted."

Tilly stared at him as though she knew exactly what he was saying, wagging her tail at him before laying her head down on the toe of his shoe. She fell asleep there, warmed by the fire, leaving Avery alone again with just his thoughts. It got tiresome, just thinking all day and talking to a dog, but he was alive, and he wasn't totally alone. Human companionship was something he missed and was severely lacking, but he was always reminding himself of how much worse it could be.

"I did everything I could think of to get ready for this," he said finally, just talking to nothing now. He stared into the woods as he spoke, thinking he might spot a deer or maybe a rabbit. "There isn't a single other thing I really could have done. I got us food, I got us blankets and clothes. I got warm boots, got shells for the gun, and have plenty of medicine and supplies. I know that it's going to get colder, but we're going to save the gas as long as we can. For the nights we can't stand it when it's bad. I don't want to run out early and be left with nothing at all."

That was one of Avery's biggest worries, the thing that lingered on his mind the most. Nights here could get brutal unless it was a mild winter, and this one wasn't starting off mild at all. If this was any indication of what was coming it would worsen, and that meant the temperature would drop more and more. He didn't know how much gas was in the big tank out back, though he had found the last receipt of sale inside, and it had been filled not long before the outbreak had begun in preparation for last winter. With nobody there to run the office the heat had never been turned on that winter, which meant the tank was probably full or at least close to it. That meant that heat was an option when things got unbearable, and he just hoped he'd know when that would be.

He didn't want to freeze to death here, trapped inside this place with his poor dog, who would have no one to care for her if he was gone. The thought of it terrified him, keeping him up at night to constantly check the temperature to see if it might be time. So far it hadn't been, but this snowstorm had been a wakeup call.

Winter was no longer this thing that lay somewhere ahead, something to prepare and plan for. It was here, the time for preparation was over, and they were in the thick of it. What had been done had to be enough going forward, because there would be no more trips to town or runs for supplies. They needed to lay low, conserve the gas they had for the vehicles, so they could have options when spring broke.

That was another thing that Avery was constantly considering, the idea of what came next. They couldn't live here forever, it wasn't meant to be like that and he wouldn't let it be. If they survived this winter, the odds were that they would not survive a second, which meant they had to get out of here. His original plan had been to head south, and that was a plan that was worth sticking with. The particulars changed now and then, mostly the location he was aiming for, but he wanted to use this winter to solidify that. They would be stuck out here just getting by and working on the plan would give him something to do. He would pick a destination and start plotting out the best route and some alternatives just in case the main way was impassable. He would make lists of supplies they would need to get before they could set out, mostly cans of spare gas and food to get them through. He had found some vehicles that would make more sense than the Camaro, smaller rigs that wouldn't hold nearly as much in the way of supplies but that would be way easier on gas.

Once they got somewhere new, the rest would be relatively easy by comparison. He could scavenge for food and supplies when they got there and scouting a place to live would be easy too. There would be all sorts of abandoned places to choose from, everything from single family homes to entire resort hotels. He could take his pick. Without winter to contend with they could grow a garden, hunt, and not have to worry about things like staying warm. It would be hotter in the summer, sure, but he'd rather contend with the heat than the cold any day of the week.

It was just a matter of getting there, of thawing out once this was through. As though reading his mind, the wind kicked up a bit, blowing snow into their little covered area. The fire was almost gone now anyway, so Avery leaned down to gather up the dog, heading back inside. He shut the door and then found his hammer and some tacks, nailing up a blanket over the door as he had planned the night before. He tucked it in at the bottom, so they could still come and go without undoing it every time, checking that the door was locked. He knew they wouldn't be going out again for anything, not even for water since he had plenty from his last trip down into the creek.

Carefully he uncovered one of the windows to let in some light, and then he got down the road atlas he'd gotten during one of his last trips to the gas station. He flipped it open and began looking at all the options they had, slipping his boots off and putting on a pair of thick slippers instead. He laid down on the air bed as he studied their choices, flopped over the side with the book resting on the floor.

"What do you think today, Till? Louisiana still? Yeah, I like that too. Maybe close to Baton Rouge or somewhere further out. I don't think New Orleans would be good at all; there was a lot going on there toward the end. That's where the guy lived who got sick first, that pig farmer, so maybe Louisiana is a bad idea," he mused out loud, still studying the more southern states on the map. "Georgia would be pretty nice too, or Mississippi. Maybe near the river so we can fish. It's a hard choice, especially since we have no way to learn about these places anymore. We just sort of have to hope and guess that it's pretty nice."

He ran his index fingers over the names of big cities and small towns, tracing roads down to them from the nearby highway. Louisiana still felt appealing despite the poor pig farmer's demise, but it was much further away. Georgia and South Carolina seemed good too, especially all those coastal towns where he could grow food and fish all year. There were pros and cons to every single place, and none of them felt any better or worse than the others.

Sometime later he put the atlas away and picked up his book, reading for a while. The wind had died down, but the temperature had taken another dip. He eventually did light one of the small space heaters and turned it down low, emitting just enough heat near their nest that it made them both a slight bit more comfortable. When reading felt too tedious he did another count of his stockpile out of sheer habit, writing down numbers that almost exactly matched those of the last count he had done.

"We may as well have an early dinner and just call it a day," Avery told the dog after a while of pacing around, peering out windows and checking the time. It was still early, but it was too cold to go outside, and he didn't feel like doing much of anything else. He turned off the little heater and got out the camp stove, hooking it up to the same little gas tank. He used it to heat up a half a can of vegetable soup, giving Tilly all the little cubes of meat out of it while he ate the rest. He kept the other half a can for the morning and put away everything after cleaning up, taking off his jeans, and climbing back into the bed.

"How did people do this in the olden days?" He mused,

staring up at the dark ceiling while letting out a heavy sigh. "I don't get it at all. I mean I know they did chores and stuff outside even when it was cold, but still. I don't know how anybody ever did this day after day, all winter long. I swear I'll go crazy."

Rolling over on his side he reached for the radio and turned it on, flipping through the stations. He held out hope that one day he'd turn it on and a voice would be there, another human reaching out looking for fellow survivors. Tonight, like every other night, there was nothing but static as he turned the dial across all the channels and came up with nothing. He flicked it off again and put his hands over his eyes, taking a moment to get his emotions under control. He would not let himself fall into deep despair, would not let himself long for the way things had been before.

"There's no going back," he whispered, speaking to himself as the beagle turned circles beneath the covers and then dropped into her spot. "I'm here, and that's all behind me. I can't keep thinking about it because it doesn't matter anymore. Jessa is gone, dad is gone, and so is mom. It's just me now, me and Till, and that's all there is in the world. I gotta keep going; I gotta do my best, because I promised I would. It can't be different; it won't be different; there is. Nothing. Else."

He fell back into sleep despite not being tired, still whispering that mantra under his breath.

There is nothing else.

TEN

ONE WEEK INTO THE TRUE START OF WINTER AVERY began to go stir crazy. He knew that was an exceptionally bad sign, especially when you considered that winter was going to drag on for a few months before spring would show itself again. He couldn't help it though, the post office starting to feel immensely small now that he had nowhere else to go. Before the snow had started to fly he had gotten out every day, either checking houses around his old neighborhood for anything that might prove useful or taking the car out to the gas station and closed up businesses near the interstate. His trips into town had been less frequent, but they had certainly been a better alternative to this.

Outside, the snow lay in soft drifts against the side of the building, more of the white stuff falling from the sky overhead. He spent as much time as he could beneath the makeshift canopy he'd strung up using the tarp, keeping a fire going whenever he was out there. Sometimes it was simply too windy to take, while other times the temperature dipped just a little bit too low. It was good for him, and Tilly too, to get out as much as possible though and he knew after a certain point they may not go out at all for days at a time. He had to play it safe no matter how cooped up he felt, and he kept reminding himself that winter didn't last forever.

Snow and frigid temperatures, like everything else in life, eventually came to an end. He just had to reach way down deep inside to find enough patience to get there, and he was trying his best. The trouble was that he had never been an exceptionally patient person, and even those hard times hadn't squashed that totally out of him.

He sat outside in his folding lawn chair stirring the coals in the fire pit with a metal poker he'd lifted from a nearby house that had a fireplace in it. There was a bubbling pot of broccoli and cheddar soup simmering, the smell making his stomach growl a little. He hadn't eaten much breakfast, slow to get moving that morning because it had been too cold to go any faster. Even Tilly, who usually didn't show a lot of interest in people food, sniffed the air and licked her chops. That made him laugh, reaching down to rub a hand over her head.

"I'll share, I promise. I think we could both use a hot meal today," he told her with a nod, lifting the pot off the grate. He got his bowl, poured himself a hearty portion, and then put the rest into her food tin. He mixed it with some dry dog food and gave it to her hot, watching the steam rise into the cold air. The beagle lapped cautious at the hot liquid, wrinkling her nose against the steam. "It'll cool fast out here, I promise. It's too cold for anything to stay hot for long."

He crumbled a couple of stale saltine crackers into his own

soup and took a bite, promptly burning his tongue. He felt stupid for chastising the dog about it when he had done the very same thing, and worse was that he knew better. He was more careful the next time, blowing on it cautiously before he took another bite.

"Tomorrow is tuna fish," he decided, knowing that Tilly didn't particularly care about his food choices but telling her anyway. "We have a bunch of canned tuna, and a few salmon too. I even found some sardines, but we'll consider those our last resort. They're the kind in mustard so it's probably tolerable, but I'm still not in a hurry to get to those yet."

Tilly was busily lapping up her meal, seemingly grateful for the warm soup in her stomach. The fire felt nice, and for this little moment in time Avery felt satisfied. It was snowing, sure, and it was definitely cold, but it could have been worse. This was tolerable, survivable, and it made him feel more confident in how things were going to go. There was no perfect formula to this at all, but he'd cracked at least part of the code and that was enough to boost him up a bit.

Finishing their meal he used fresh snow to scrub out the bowl, clean the spoon, and then returned everything back inside to their proper places. By the time he finished up the fire was burning low and the wind was kicking up a bit, so he decided it was time to move inside. He pulled in his chair and tucked it into the corner, shedding his boots so he didn't drip water. He used an old towel to dry off Tilly's paws and then he shut up the door, sequestering them away again.

"I wish we had more days like this. Mild ones, ones where we don't have to stay inside so much and can get fresh air. Maybe I can draw up some ideas for building a sled I can pull, and then we can at least venture a little bit further out away from the building and cut some more wood. There's plenty, but we can keep an outside fire going nearly all the time with more wood. Or maybe I can get some stove pipe and make some sort of vent in here and then we can try and snag us a little wood stove in one of these old houses. If we could vent it and get enough wood, we wouldn't be cold at all this winter. I should have thought of that before! Why didn't I? I'm so stupid!"

Tilly had no answer for him, climbing onto their bed and turning around three times before flopping down with a sigh. Avery dropped down onto a bean bag chair he'd snagged several weeks prior, stretching out his legs and groaning quietly. He really did wish he had already thought about trying to create some sort of venting for a wood stove, though in reality he knew it was a stupid idea. Stoves were heavy, and there was likely no way he'd be able to move one on his own. It would have been nice though, something that he could use all winter long without fear of running out of fuel. Wood was abundant, he could find enough dead stuff likely to see him through, but there was no point in being upset about it now.

Opening his eyes, he stared up at the one uncovered window, high up near the ceiling, providing a view of the gray sky, some treetops, and nothing else. It let in enough light to throw some shadows along the wall, the shadows moving more and more as the wind picked up. When would this be over? When would there be another sunny, mild day? His heart started to beat harder in his chest and bile rose in his throat, sitting suddenly upright and shaking out his hands which had started to tingle.

The panic attack came on hard and fast, though he knew

immediately what it was. He'd been having them for ages, even before his mother had died, and this one was squeezing him tightly. He felt like he couldn't breathe, hands pressing to his chest where he felt his heart beating wildly like it was trying to escape his rib cage. The room felt like it was closing in on him, those shadows reaching and reaching in an effort to grab him. He had never been claustrophobic before but he felt it now, trapped inside this rickety old post office with its cold and dampness trying to suffocate him.

Leaving the warm nest, Tilly came to him and whined pitifully as she pawed at his leg. Avery reached out for her, sinking his shaking fingers into her warm fur. The beagle laid her head on his knee and tried to comfort him through it, and when it was finally over he felt insanely exhausted.

"We have to get out of here, Tilly. We can't wait forever, as soon as winter is over we have to go. I can't just keep talking about it either, like it really has to happen. We can't live in this drafty old dump forever, we have to find a place where we can stay forever. A good place, a place that isn't so hard."

He ached all over, and he hoped it was just from the sudden panic and not from the possibility of getting sick. He did let himself take two Tylenol with a swig of cold water before he crawled to the air mattress and wrapped himself up in the covers. The dog joined him and he hugged her tight, burying his face into her fur.

"I wish mom were here," he whispered quietly as his heavy eyes fell shut. "She'd know what to do better than me. She always did."

ELEVEN

March 21st, 2018

THE POPULATION OF GRAVEN HAD CONTINUED TO dwindle slowly after the mass exodus in the fall, Avery and Jemma watching as their neighbors and friends began to disappear one by one. None of those who had left by car back in October and November returned to their homes, all those houses just sitting vacant and empty through the dreary months of winter. There were a few homes, including their own, that had still shown signs of life until recently. One by one doors closed and nobody came outside again, or where there had been smoke curling from a chimney there was now nothing at all.

Their small rural neighborhood had become a graveyard of sorts, and it made Avery break out in goosebumps every time he thought about it. He and his mother often talked about plundering the empty houses, or the houses where there were only the dead now, but they hadn't yet. They kept putting it off, waiting until that moment when they were desperate enough. It hadn't come yet but it was getting close, and they both knew it. Despite there being only two of them the stores in the cellar and in the pantry were growing thinner, and neither of them had the hunting prowess that Telford had possessed. Time would eventually force them to do things they didn't necessarily want to do, but they weren't rushing it.

The winter hadn't been as bad as it might have been on them, just a few heavy snows and one substantial storm. They had alternated between heating with wood and with electricity, growing scared of the possibility of the power going and not coming back. It had started flickering off and on at random in December, and once or twice had gone out for a few hours at a stretch. It had always come back on, but that too was for a limited amount of time much like everything else. Without people running the plants and keeping things on the up, all the previously vital services were bound to fail.

"We just have to think of it like an adventure," Jemma told him time and again, as though she could make him not panic by treating it like something it wasn't. Avery was careful to never tell her that he was old enough to know better, because he was, but instead just let her carry on. It made her feel better, and hurting her feelings was the last thing he wanted to do.

They ate small, well planned out meals as spring finally broke and the world began to properly thaw out. They continued boiling well water after finally drinking the bottled stuff from the cellar now that Telford wasn't around to insist they didn't. What was the point in hanging onto it? It wasn't like they'd be any better or worse off.. The world was in about as dire straits as it could get without catching fire. So they had indulged and divided it up, making it last as long as possible which hadn't been nearly long enough.

It was after the last of the snow had melted and the spring rains set in that Jemma had broken the bad news to Avery. They were dredging the bottom of the barrel with their rations, and so something had to be done. She was too wary of going into town; they weren't sure anymore what it was like or if there were any people around, and instead lobbied to try some of the neighboring houses. Avery hated the idea of it and vehemently refused, insisting instead on attempting to catch some food in the woods. They saw plenty of wildlife, which didn't seem to be impacted at all by Ruger, and he had Tilly who could surely do some tracking. She was a beagle, after all, and wasn't that their job?

His mother seemed cross at the idea but let him go anyway, carrying his father's shotgun with the safety on. As he trudged up into the woods behind their house, the dog right at his heels, his mother took it upon herself to try her own approach. She waited for Avery to be well out of sight before grabbing an old backpack and heading next door to the Smith's house.

It had been sitting empty the longest of any other home on their road, ever since the day the emergency team had come for Nellie and Jamie. She assumed that they hadn't been able to take everything in their cupboards and she was at least a little bit right, able to snag a few cans before realizing she had to move on. She tried some of the other houses that had been simply abandoned but found them all locked up, as though the fleeing owners thought they would be returning to them when this was all over. The thought made her laugh, a bitter and hollow sound, because there was no way anyone would be coming back here.

Finally she let herself into the Martin home, a large old place with a wrap-around porch and a classic pickup truck sitting in the driveway. The Martin's, Ellen and Raleigh, were an elderly couple who were always good to their neighbors. They had paid Avery five bucks a week for the past three summers to mow their lawn, and always gave him fresh cookies before sending him home with his pay. For a while she and her son had tried to check up on them as best as they could manage, but neither Ellen nor Raleigh had been seen or heard from for a couple of months.

As soon as she got in the door Jemma's fears were confirmed, a horrible smell assaulting her senses. She pulled her shirt up over her nose and mouth, making her way carefully through the dark house. She saw nothing in the living room or hallway, and the kitchen was just as empty as the other rooms. That meant that the Martin's were likely upstairs, which was just as well. Jemma knew enough without having to see anything, just wanting to find what she had come for and to get back out again quickly.

This time she hit more of a jackpot, emptying the contents of several cabinets into her bag. There were canned soups and vegetables, packets of Ramen noodles in several flavors, and packages of beef jerky. She checked the pantry and found it mostly bare, though she did nab an unopened but out of date bag of chips, and some cookie dough mix she thought she could improvise enough to make them a treat.

Peering into the fridge, Jemma saw a square, refillable water container that was completely full and sitting alone on the bottom shelf. It was warm, sure, but judging by the amount of water it held it had most likely not been used. She hefted it out and put it on the counter, grabbing a glass from the cabinet. She turned the lever on the spout and good, clear water filled up the glass. She gave it a sniff, determined it was clean, and took a sip. It tasted fine to her, and she finished the rest of the glass in couple of deep swallows.

The container was too big for her to carry all the way home on her own, so she left it out with the idea of coming back for it later. She and Avery could return with the wagon and pull it back home, where they could use it up in place of their well water. Anything that could be useful should be used, and it was always a good idea to keep fresh water on hand. The less they had to draw from the well and boil, the better.

Needing fresh air and having a great desire to get out of a house that contained the heaviness of death, Jemma went out through the back door. She listened for Avery and Tilly but heard nothing, making her way back across the sloping hillside to their own house. She stored away her spoils and then washed her hands, settling down with an old seed catalog to try and get some ideas for planting a fresh garden. They had saved seeds from last year's bounty, and they needed a good garden now more than ever.

She was still there when Avery turned at dusk, empty-handed and filthy dirty. Tilly was exhausted and immediately went to her dog bed, dropping onto it without doing her usual three spins. He declined to talk about the failed hunting experiment, opting instead to clean up and change his clothes while she got dinner going.

Jemma fixed two packets of Ramen noodles, chicken flavored, as a surprise and had the steaming bowls already on the table when Avery returned. He was so hungry and so elated at the treat that he began to eat without considering where it had come from, halfway done with his portion before he thought to ask.

"Mom, we didn't have this down in the cellar with the other stuff. Where did you get packaged noodles from? Did you go into town? I thought you were afraid to do that," Avery asked, eyes wide with curiosity as he took another bite. "You should have told me, we could have gone together!"

"I didn't go to town," Jemma said simply, stirring her noodles around before taking a small bite. "I didn't go that far."

Realization began to dawn as Avery stared at his mother across the small kitchen table, fork still in hand with a healthy mouthful of noodles twirled around the prongs. He let out a sharp breath of disbelief, shaking his head at her. "Mom! I told you not to do that," he chastised her, putting his fork back down a little harder than he intended to. "It's like...it's like stealing! It doesn't matter if the world is ending, that doesn't make it right! Worse, it's like grave robbing!"

Jemma knew that persuasion would likely not work in this scenario, so she didn't even try. Instead she just used her own logic and the facts of the situation which was the best course of action. "Avery, listen to me. Those people are either gone and we don't know what became of them, or they are dead and not in need of this stuff anymore. Okay? It isn't stealing if that's the case, because they're gone and this stuff would just sit and rot. It's better that we have it and use it, that we keep ourselves from starving. I don't think Mr. and Mrs. Martin would want to know that you starved to death when there was perfectly good food sitting right in their unused kitchen."

"You got this from the Martin's?" Avery asked, his lips pursed so hard they practically disappeared. "So they're both dead then? Oh man. Oh man."

"Avery, I promise that you're making it more of a deal than it really has to be. Yes, I took this from the Martin's and, yes, they are deceased now. They're gone, and I would rather take this stuff from people who we liked and cared about, and who cared about us, than let something happen to you. I'm sorry if you can't see it that way now, but you're going to have to if we're going to keep ourselves afloat. I know you have a soft heart, but there are times when you have to be tough and put up a hard exterior and this is one of those times. Survival isn't for the soft-hearted, okay? You have to try and understand that."

Avery just stared at his mother for another beat longer and then nodded, picking his fork back up. He took a bite and just ate in silence for a bit, silently mulling things over. He knew she wasn't wrong, even if he very much did not like it, and anyway it couldn't be taken back now. Returning the food would be pointless, and she was right in that the Martin's didn't need it anymore, no matter how he felt about the situation.

"I guess this is better than waiting on me to catch something while hunting," he finally consented, giving his mom a tiny smile. That made Jemma smile in return, relief washing over her that he wasn't going to keep being upset about things.

This was not a world made for feeling guilty about every little thing you did. This was a world that was going to push them all to change in unexpected ways. It would push young men like Avery to grow up faster than anticipated, and they were all going to learn lessons in survival. Getting upset wouldn't make a bit of difference either, because what had to be would be no matter what.

Dinner was at least more satisfying than usual, and they cleaned up together before drifting to the living room. Avery sprawled on the floor with his head on a throw pillow, reading a comic book that he'd found in the attic while they were sorting out possible supplies. Jemma sat down on the sofa to work on crocheting a blanket she had started before Ruger had ravaged the world, figuring that the focus was good for her and would at least keep her mind off other things.

Two hours passed in relative silence, Avery dozing on the floor with the dog while Jemma put away her crocheting and considered heating up enough water for a proper bath. She was still considering it when the lights dimmed and then surged several times, finally deciding to stay on at least for the moment. Her head was tilted to the side and she was staring at the floor lamp in the far corner when her throat began to tickle so badly she had to give in to the undeniable urge to cough. She put her hand over her mouth out of instinct, the tickle still lingering despite her best attempt to clear her throat.

The tickle and the gentle cough associated with throat clearing became something else very quickly, her other hand against her chest as she began to cough outright. It was a deep cough, the kind that hurts in your chest, and though the tickle did fade away the cough remained. She left the living room to get a glass of water, taking a few long drinks to soother her throat and to hopefully solve the problem.

Only it didn't. The cold water felt nice, sure, but the cough kept on persisting. She didn't feel like that bath now, calling out to Avery that she was going to lie down. Jemma disappeared up the stairs before he could get himself up off the living room floor, slipping into her bedroom and shutting the door.

Avery felt worried, able to hear her relentless hacking even downstairs. He locked up the house and shut off most of the lights, drifting up after her and listening at her door. He stayed there for a while, unsure of what he could do to help; only heading into his own room when things seemed to get calmer and quieter. He left his door open so he could hear her better if she called him and lay down to sleep, not stirring again until well into the morning.

"Mom," Avery called out the moment his feet hit the floor, heading across the hall to her still shut bedroom door. "Mom!"

When Jemma didn't answer Avery tried the knob and found it unlocked, shoving his way inside. His mother was still in the bed wearing a tank top and a pair of shorts, hugging her arms around a pillow. She was coughing into it to muffle the sound, her forehead dotted with sweat. They hadn't used any heat the night before and he thought it was a little cool himself, but she was clearly burning up. That was when the worry really hit him, hurrying over and reaching out to touch her forehead for a test.

Jemma, sick as she looked, reacted by scooting away from him fast. She sat upright in the middle of the bed, and in the filtered light shining through the gauzy window curtains Avery could see now how pallid she looked. "Don't touch me," she told him, voice stern but also a bit shaky. "I'm sick, Avery, and I don't want you near me. I don't want to give this to you, we got lucky before with Jessa but lightning won't strike twice. Just go downstairs and stay there, do you hear me?"

"No way," Avery told her, shaking his head adamantly. What he really wanted to do was cry, to totally break down, but he couldn't do that. Not yet anyway, not while she was there to see it and to feel guilty for it. That could come later. For now he had to help her. "I'm not leaving you, mom. You didn't leave Jess, and I'm not doing that either."

There was a short pause and then he frowned hard, wringing his hands. "Mom....you went over to the Martin's yesterday, into their house. It's been all closed up for a while, and we don't know for sure but they probably died from being sick. You went in there where there were all sorts of germs in a place that wasn't cleaned up or aired out. I...I'm sure that's where you got it. There's no other real answer, unless it's really in the water and we haven't been careful enough."

"I know, I thought of that last night, but I don't think that's how I got it. I think...it was water from their fridge. It was in a big, reusable container, and I drank some of it assuming it was clean. It could have been untreated well water though, they got water from the same stream as us," Jemma admitted, brushing her hair back off her damp forehead. "I really do think it was luck with Jessa, I was in that room with her and still didn't get sick. Neither did you or dad, so either we dodged a bullet or it wasn't Ruger after all. We won't ever know that now, but I do know that I don't want you getting sick. You don't have to stay here, Avery, it's okay. We know what's going to happen, there's no use in pretending otherwise."

"Nothing you say is going to make me leave," Avery told her simply, shrugging his shoulders. He pulled the armchair in the corner up to the side of the bed, easing himself into it. "You need cold water to drink, and a cloth for your forehead to help with the fever. You're running a fever now, right?"

"I haven't checked it to see how high, but yes. The fever started a couple of hours ago," Jemma acknowledged, though it was clear she was a little loathe to admit it to him. "Water would be nice, but no food. The thought of eating makes me feel nauseous; I don't want to spend what time I have left throwing up in a bucket."

Avery made a few trips downstairs, getting her cold water to drink and wetting two cloths, one for her forehead and one for the back of her neck. He read to her from a book while she tried to nap, Tilly joining them and laying on the bed at Jemma's feet. The fever grew steadily worse, and despite not eating she threw up several times and then dry-heaved painfully when there was nothing else to come up. He made more trips to dispose of the waste in the bucket and to wet the cloths again in an effort to bring her comfort.

It all felt very surreal, the hours melting together as the day wore into the night again. Jemma slept fitfully and Avery napped when he could, catching ten minutes here or twenty minutes there. They had two good hours over the course of the night where they both slept, getting some real rest before things got considerably worse near dawn.

Jemma woke up Avery up moaning in agony, her mouth dry and her body aching. He gave her a drink and she strangled on it, coughing and hacking as she struggled to catch her breath. He hit her on the back and she finally threw up, all over her legs and the bedclothes. Tilly had long since left, pacing in the hallway outside and whining pitifully as Avery did everything he could.

The first seizure like episode happened around eight, and then the second one at ten. Her body just went rigid and her teeth clacked together, a horrible sound that he knew he'd never forget. A wrist to her forehead told Avery that the fever was raging, likely causing the episodes, but at one that afternoon it all came to a very sudden end. He was holding onto her hand as she had another violent seizure, sucking in deep breaths that made her lungs rattle a little. Her breaths were wheezy at best and she kept clutching at her throat, and then suddenly her body went rigid and her eyes rolled back.

That was it. That was all there was and then it was over, the house going eerily silent save for the clock on the wall counting down the useless minutes. Jemma laid stiff, her hand still in Avery's and her eyes staring blankly up at the ceiling. Her mouth was partially open and her teeth were clenched together tightly, the scent of death already permeating the room. Avery pulled his fingers from hers and stood up, shaking as he left the room quickly and pulled the door closed behind him. He sat down at the top of the stairs and began to cry, hugging Tilly when she wiggled her way into his lap.

"We're alone here now," he whispered against the top of her head, which was wrinkled with worry. "It's just us now. Oh God, Tilly! What are we going to do? There has to be somebody, right? We can't be it."

Spurred by a sudden panic, Avery rose to his feet and let the beagle slide off his lap. He rushed down the stairs and outside to the front porch, where he began to scream. His voice echoed off the hills and through the trees, carrying it to anyone within hearing distance.

"HELP! ANYONE! IS THERE SOMEONE ELSE? PLEASE!"

Nobody came. No heads poked out of opened doors or windows, no neighbors hurried out to placate him. If there was anyone they weren't in Graven, too far away to hear or help him. They were really and truly alone now, and it felt for a moment like the whole world was collapsing in. How was someone just the last person alive? How was it that he had somehow ended up in this situation? It didn't make any sense, nothing did, and trying to rationalize it just somehow made it all worse.

Avery sat down on the porch swing and rocked slowly back and forth, getting a game plan together in his head. Odds were that his second round of exposure would be the last, and he'd probably start falling ill by that night. Some folks took a little longer to get sick, a couple of days even, and he knew that he could not spend another night in this house no matter what. He'd lost his sister, father, and mother here and the idea of lying down to sleep in it again was unbearable. That was the thought that finally got him moving, spurring him into real action instead of letting him continue to wallow.

He started with the cellar, moving all the provisions into the back of his sister's old red wagon. There wasn't much to take in the way of food, so everything fit well and he wouldn't have to make multiple trips. Inside he got the air mattress and pump from the hall closet, along with some sheets and the pillows from his own bed. He got the shotgun and the few shells there were left, and then the radio that could run on either electricity or batteries. He got a few things from the fridge, primarily the already boiled containers of well water, and then he grabbed a couple of picture albums that he wanted to keep for sentimental value. Even if he did die, maybe someone would find them in the future so they would at least not be totally forgotten.

With everything stacked in the wagon, he pulled it all away

from the house and left it there for later. He broke open the tool shed out back, not interested in hunting for the key, and found the half-empty can of lawn mower gas and the small container of kerosene stored on a shelf. He went through the house room by room, spreading the flammable liquids around so that things would burn more efficiently. He saved the upstairs master bedroom for last, using what was left to douse his mother's body. He didn't look back as he left the room, tossing the canister aside.

Avery lit the fire from outside the front door, listening to the somewhat satisfying whoosh of air as the flame hit the gas. It took of fast, spreading faster than he had imagined possible. The fire raced up the stairs and all through the rooms, burning hot and fast. He grabbed Tilly and backed up out onto the lawn, watching as the fire began to consume the home of his childhood, the house he had grown up in and where his family had left him.

He knew it would likely spread through the neighborhood, jump from house to house, but what did it matter? It wasn't like anyone was there. Hell, it wasn't like anyone was anywhere.

Watching the fire until the top portion of the house began to cave in; Avery finally gathered up Tilly and the wagon and set off down the hill. He got to the road and just stood looking around in the dim light of evening, trying to decide where to go. He knew which houses had been abandoned and which likely held the dead, but it felt wrong to stay in someone's home regardless. His eyes lit on the small, square building across the bridge and he headed that way instead.

The old post office had been abandoned a long time ago now, closing up not too long after the Ruger virus had begun to spread in earnest. Scientists had been worried that terrorist groups would try and spread the virus somehow, like they had spread anthrax around once upon time, and they didn't want to risk it. So mail service had closed down, which was just as well. Who wanted to get sale papers and credit card offers when the world was ending? It was all pointless, and nobody had kicked up much fuss about it.

When the postmaster had abandoned ship they had at least locked up, and Avery finally had to use a crowbar to pry open one of the old windows at the back of the building. He finally got it open enough to shimmy through, dropping Tilly in first before he joined her. Despite having been closed for a year or more the place wasn't so bad. It just smelled a little musty and needed to be aired out. He unlocked the back door and pulled in his wagon, getting out the air mattress and the pump. The place still had working power so he didn't have to blow the thing up by hand, sliding it into a corner after putting on the fitted sheet.

"Just for tonight," he told Tilly, finding a jar of maraschino cherries in the wagon of meager provisions. He opened those up and ate a few, taking a swig of the sweet juice they floated in before sealing up the jar again. He drank some water and poured some into an old bowl he'd grabbed for Tilly, promising to get her some dog food the next day.

"Mom did it, right?" He asked into the growing darkness, stretched out on his makeshift bed with his shoes off. Through the windows the glow of the still burning fire cast shadows on the ceiling, and he watched them dancing with a strange sort of detachment. "She went into the houses and she got stuff, so why can't we? It might not even matter anyway, when the cough comes it's over for me. If that happens then I'll let you out, so you can be free in the wild. People say domesticated dogs can't survive on their own, but I think you can, Tilly. Those instincts will come back, I'm pretty sure of it. I just know I have to give you a fair shake."

So that was what Avery decided to do, so mentally and physically exhausted that he fell into a deep sleep nearly immediately. Outside the frogs had started to croak their night songs, back in action now that the weather was warming up, and he lay on his back with the blanket tucked beneath him and his beagle resting her head on his stomach. As he slept the fire began to burn out, though the coals and remnants of the house would stay hot and smoldering for days after. The wind had been low so it hadn't spread as he had imagined it would, though it didn't matter. One house or ten houses, they were empty now and would likely always be that way.

Avery dreamed of nothing, or at least nothing that he could remember when morning came which was just as well. Any dreams that visited him would likely have been nightmares, and he had been shaken up enough by the real world. He didn't need dreams to remind him of what horrors lingered. Monsters could no longer frighten him anyway.

When he woke up he felt good, aside from his eyes being slightly puffy from all the smoke from the fire. He hadn't coughed at all, and he had no fever. Incubation varied though, and he wouldn't call himself okay until at least seventy-two hours passed which would come and go as he busied himself with stocking up on essentials. Food was the direst need he had, followed by a good water source, and then other necessary supplies. He hadn't thought to grab the little things, like pain relievers or band aids, which were things that he felt the sudden urge to have on hand. He found some paper and a couple of pens and began to make lists, the first of which was dog food for his loyal companion.

The cough wouldn't come, nor would the fever. Instead of waiting to die he continued to live, counting down the days one by one. He made trips to places just down the road first, then the gas station by the highway, and finally to town. He daydreamed of going somewhere new, of trying to find other people like him. People who were seemingly immune, people who had been passed over by the clutches of death brought on the heels of the Ruger virus.

People who would want to build a community, work together, and continue to survive. It would work this way for a little while, that much he knew, but not forever. So he began to dream of going south, to warmer climates. He'd give himself a year, just one, to make a plan and stick with it. Living was now just about more than staying alive, it was everything.

There was nothing but him, his dog, and a very primal need for survival and nothing more.

TWELVE

THE SNOW BEGAN TO FALL AGAIN HEAVILY, AFTER A few days of melting that had allowed Avery to get out and about a little more. He'd cut some more wood for the stack by the back door, and he'd attempted to set some snares to try and catch a rabbit. Those had turned up empty, but it had been nice enough just getting outside to even try. He thought briefly about making another run to town to try and get into the public library again, wondering if he might find some books to teach him some more practical skills. He wanted to learn to sew, as he had some clothes that were becoming in dire need of repair, and he figured it couldn't hurt to start reading up more on gardening. It was still a long way to spring, but if he started working now he'd be better prepared.

With fresh snow on, though, it was back to staying close to home, going out only to cook under his little lean-to and then right back in again. There was a biting wind now, and it was too hard to dry out any clothing that got wet so he tried to keep that to a minimum. He did have a good stockpile of reading material, and all his maps so he could work on his plan for what would happen come spring. It wasn't the worst setup in the world, and even though he vehemently wished he could be outside more it could have been much worse.

For the first time, he had to use the furnace too, the temperature dipping so low that no amount of clothing layered on was going to do the trick. He moved the air mattress a little closer to the big grate on the floor near the front of the office. He was careful not to let anything touch the metal of the grate in case it got too hot and melted or started an accidental fire. He had turned the thing on but kept the temperature as low as he could get away with, which was plenty enough laying so close. He slept well that night, truly warm and toasty for the first time in a long time, though he did hope the temperature would rise again soon so he didn't use up too much gas.

There were dreary, overcast snow days mixed with sunny temperate ones, par for the course for this time of year. He thought about how Christmas was getting nearer and nearer, marking the days on a calendar on the wall, and it made him feel a little melancholy. Last Christmas had been hard, the worst of his life, but he had at least had his mother. Now he had nobody but Tilly, and while he loved her dearly things would just never be the same. What was the point of even thinking about things like holidays now that there was just him? There was nothing to celebrate, nothing to look forward to, and so he tried to put it out of his mind.

More and more he also thought about what had happened to

his mother, to Jessa, and to his father. They would never know if his dad would have gotten sick or not; he hadn't wanted to find out and so he had prevented it from becoming a possibility. Jessa was the youngest, the weakest, and she had been the first to go. A lot of children and the very elderly had been first, so she fit a certain demographic he supposed and had most likely gotten it from a minute amount of bacteria in the well water. His mother hadn't gotten sick after taking care of Jessa, so why had she gotten sick after going into the Martin's house? It seemed so impossible, but he supposed that was what made it so awful. There didn't have to be a rhyme or reason with this sort of thing, and that just added to the terror of it all.

When Jessa had gotten sick the virus wasn't raging nearly as badly, not to mention they had all just been healthier then. They were still eating pretty good, still taking their daily medications that hadn't run out yet, and his mother had taken several. She'd had high blood pressure, for one, and suffered from an autoimmune disease as well, a strange stomach thing that Avery had never been able to spell or properly pronounce. It was possible that as time had passed and food had been more meager and there was no more medication to help keep her well that her body had simply become unable to ward the virus off. It wasn't an unheard-of situation, and while Avery wasn't sure about the facts it made sense to him just the same.

"What about me then?" He asked out loud, stretched out on his stomach across the air bed. He'd left it near the heat grate in the floor, figuring there was no use in moving it every single time he had to use the heater. This would be fine for now, and maybe even better since he was further away from the drafty windows and corners. "Why didn't I ever get sick? I've been in plenty of sick houses now, seen bodies up close, but I'm still perfectly fine. Boiling the water every day, but still drinking it. So why not me?"

The theories on this were severely limited, with only a handful of conclusions to work with at best. There was the possibility that his own immune system was just that good, able to ward off the virus for the time being. If that were true then the facts would change as food ran short and he was less and less able to keep up his strength. At that point the Ruger virus was more likely to work its way into his body and finally kill him, but he wasn't so sure about that. He hadn't really been any better off than his mom a few months ago, save for just maybe being in slightly better health, so he didn't think that was it.

The most likely scenario he could think up was that he was probably somehow, someway, immune. There had never been any mentions on the news, television or radio, about people coming up immune to the virus. Then again that probably hadn't been known at the time, or at least not a possibility that was currently being considered. It explained why he hadn't gotten ill when Jessa had, or why he'd scraped by when taking care of his mother too. He'd come in plenty of contact with Ruger, and had still managed to walk away perfectly well after each encounter. Immunity made sense, and he wondered too if maybe his father had also been immune. Such things were probably genetic in nature, but that was just another thing to never find out. His dad had made his choices, just as Avery had made his, and some things were just not meant to be known.

If he was truly immune, something he didn't know for sure, that meant he'd never get sick. Or, at least, that he'd never get sick with the Ruger virus. Everything else, including the regular flu, could still get him. It was a strange prospect to imagine, the world gone and him left behind, immune to the disease that had wiped out mankind. Those thoughts were probably silly though, there was likely someone else somewhere out there who was the same as him. Another immune person who had managed to get passed over, or maybe there was someone hiding in a fallout shelter just waiting for the proverbial smoke to clear before coming back to the surface.

Those thoughts didn't linger long though, and they didn't tend to stick with him. Even if there were others, or at least one another, he was pretty certain that they weren't here, not in Graven, and not in the neighboring area. The odds had to be pretty slim, based on mere statistics alone.

"Ugh, stop thinking about it," he grumbled to himself as he got up, grabbing a can of Vienna sausages and some more stale crackers to have for his dinner. He made a fire outside again in the fire pit and heated the sausages up, improving their edibility only marginally. He gave the last one to Tilly, nice and warm for her, not able to get it down.

It was already growing dark outside, and he left the fire to burn on out as they headed inside. The wind was howling and shrieking again, swirling the once more falling snow this way and thought so there were near white-out conditions outside the windows. He made sure they were all covered well and then turned on his little lamp, settling in for some reading before he let himself fall asleep. He even tried the radio first, getting nothing but static as he had every night for months. He knew that there would come a day soon when he gave trying it all together, but for now the routine act of it was a small comfort.

He fell asleep without meaning to, the book resting on his chest and the room growing cold. When he was startled from sleep sometime later the kerosene lamp had burned low so the light was strange and full of shadows, the wind still screaming and shaking the old building for all it was worth. He probably wouldn't have woken to the sounds from outside at all if it hadn't been for Tilly, the beagle standing up with her nose pressed to the crack of the heavy wooden door that led from the back of the office into the lobby. He never used that entrance, and the door was always locked up tight to the outside. He did store some of his water there and things that he wanted to keep cold but planned on using soon, like unfinished food sealed in airtight containers.

Avery's first thought was that a critter had somehow gotten in and was causing some damage, Tilly waking at the noise that his human ears couldn't detect and then smelling the critter through the crack. It had been a sharp, keen beagle bark that had woken him up, but as he grabbed the lantern and approached her, he could hear now that she was growling. That was unusual, very out of character for her, but he still regarded it as some animal trying to eat their leftovers and maybe get into their water storage too. Sliding on his slippers to avoid contact with the cold lobby floor, Avery slid the bolts out of place and opened the door, peering out into the small area.

The lobby was not a big space, and he had never had much reason to utilize it. There was only the small table where people could grab different types of labels for their mail, an old antique mailbox that sat in the corner and had no key to even open it with, and then the boxes where folks could check their mail. There was a small window where people could get assistance, but he kept it closed with the bars down over it all the time to help keep out the cold that seeped in from around the door.

He took a peek saw nothing there, or at least nothing immediately noticeable. The containers of food sat on top of the counter still sealed shut, and the four jugs of clean water sat beside them with the lids still on and not leaking. The beagle scurried out ahead of him and ran to the door, baying again as her hackles went up. It occurred to him then, quite suddenly at that, that something was out there. Could an animal smell food through a door and containers like that? Could it be something like a bear wanting to get in where there was something good and free to eat?

He had been about to grab Tilly and run for it back to safety and the shotgun when he heard the noise that had roused the little beagle up in the first place. It was impossible not to hear it now, standing right on top of the door, his heart starting to pound when he recognized it for what it was. Some*one* was out there. Some*one* not some*thing*, and they were knocking rather intently on his front door.

THIRTEEN

AVERY'S FIRST INSTINCT WAS TO FLEE, TO RUN INTO the back of the building and lock tight the door that separated the lobby from the rest of the building. He started to do just that, but then his brain caught up with him and he took in a few deep, calming breaths. There was someone out there, another person who was alive and possibly well. It crossed his mind that they could be sick, but from what he had seen of the Ruger virus once you came down with the cough the fever quickly followed and rendered you more or less bedridden until the end. It was fairly unlikely that someone had wondered in from somewhere else while sick, but there was still a risk. Besides the virus they could be ill in other ways, primarily mentally, which scared him more than other possibilities.

His mind momentarily flickered to the three men he and his mother had encountered just after his father had died. One of them had been sick but still on his feet (at least until that night), and the other two had been well enough to be up to no good. Two of them were dead, but they had let the third run. What if he'd still been hanging around somewhere nearby? Avery hadn't been to every single dwelling there was between here and town, not by a long shot, and there were other hiding places besides. The situation could be potentially dangerous, in a lot of ways.

Still, it was a person. A living, breathing human like himself and they were out in the storm. Shooing Tilly back he went for the locks, holding up his lantern to try and get a better look through the panes of glass in the door. Whoever they were they had on a hood and a scarf so he couldn't see too much besides a pair of brown eyes, and the fact that they appeared smaller than he was. That solidified for him that it was not the third man from before, which was a relief, and it also meant he had an advantage if they had a tussle as he was the larger opponent. He just hoped it wouldn't come to anything like that, getting the locks undone and then stepping back as the person went for the knob.

They blew in with a burst of frigid air, pulling the door shut quickly behind them. Avery had stepped further into the lobby now, Tilly at his feet with her hackles still up. The person in front of him began to unwind the scarf around their face, and as it fell away he saw that there was a girl under those layers, with rosy cheeks and slightly glassy looking eyes. Immediately he put up a hand, a way of cautioning her against moving any closer.

"Are you sick?" He asked, knowing it had to be brought up and sooner rather than later given the circumstances. "Do you have a cough? A fever? I let you in because it's cold outside, and because I haven't seen another person in months, but if you're sick you have to go. I just want that said first and foremost."

"You're charming," the girl answered, a little breathless as she tugged off her gloves and rubbed her hands together to try and warm them up. "I'm not sick, just been trying to find someone else alive. I was up on the ridge earlier, just going house to house, and I saw your fire down here. I started walking again but it got dark and I got all turned around. I didn't think I'd ever get down here, and by the time I got to the road here the fire had gone out so it was hard to judge if I was even in the right place. Thank God I found it though, and it would really suck to be lost out there in this mess."

After a moment of consideration she held out a hand to him tentatively, offering him a hint of a smile. "I'm Krissy Rawlins," she told him with a nod of confirmation. "Nice to meet you, considering."

Avery gave her a skeptical look and then took her hand carefully in his, giving it a gentle shake. "Avery Harris. You don't have any weapons, do you? Because I don't want to get murdered in my sleep either."

This time Krissy rolled her eyes at him and then slid a backpack off one shoulder, holding it out to him. "You can check if you want. I have a pocket knife but that's about it. A few provisions, some things I picked up along the way but it isn't much. That's part of the reason why I finally left my hideout and started searching for others. It was getting too hard out there on my own, and there's not a whole lot left to pick over. I'm not going to kill you, I promise you that. I mean what would be the point? We're the last two people left, maybe anywhere so far as I can tell. It would be pretty stupid of me to kill the only company I'm likely to ever find."

"Fair point," Avery decided, unzipping the bag to peer in. He saw a packet of beef jerky, some candy bars, a few canned goods, and a large bottle of water. He zipped it back up and handed it over to her, heading through the second door and into the back area of the post office. "It's not crazy warm in here, but it's better than out there. I turned the heat on low and I sleep close to it so it helps at least a little."

Krissy seemed pleased that there was heat, sitting down on the floor by the grate and sliding off her boots, resting her feet right up against the metal. She opened her pack again and pulled out a candy bar, taking a bite as she started to warm herself up. "You've got quite the set up in here," she commented, glancing around with interest. The lamp was still burning low, so light was minimal, but it was enough. "I thought I was crazy knocking on the door here, but I saw your woodpile and everything so I figured this had to be it. Why the post office? There are loads of empty houses."

Avery was still trying to wrap his mind around another person being present, latching the middle door shut and stuffing a towel underneath it to keep out the cold from the lobby. Tilly was still observing the new person, sniffing around the girl but keeping a good bit of distance between them. He just let her pace and fret, knowing she would be a good judge of character in the end, and he'd trust her instincts over his own.

"Why not?" Avery asked, sitting down on his air mattress which squeaked beneath him as he adjusted his weight. "It's not too big, so everything I need is in close quarters with me. It has plenty of storage for food and supplies, and it's right by a running source of freshwater. It's got a toilet, gas heat, and a crawl space of sorts underneath where I could store things if need be to keep them cool. I lived nearby and when my house burnt it just felt wrong to stay in someone else's place. Even if they were dead or gone, I couldn't bring myself to do it so this was a logical choice."

"I get that," Krissy agreed, finishing off the candy bar and leaning forward to warm her hands next. "I've been staying way out by the caves, in a little log cabin I stumbled on. I started out looking for others a while ago, but walking all the time just started wearing me out. I gathered up some stuff and hid out, but when the weather started to turn and food started running out I knew I couldn't keep staying there. I figured at best I might find another survivor, and at worst I'd find a house with enough stuff to get me through and I'd have to wait for spring. I saw you though, and here I am!"

He didn't know of any cabins near the caves, unless she was talking about the ones that people could rent out and that stayed booked up for weeks and months at a time in the summer and fall. Those wouldn't have had food though, they weren't kept stocked up, so it was more likely that she had veered off some small side road and had ended up at someone's hunting shack or maybe even just a weekend place. He supposed it didn't really matter though, because she had been traveling for what sounded like quite some time and the details were probably fuzzy at best by now.

"So did you see *anyone* else at all until me?" He asked with a sinking feeling in his gut even as he asked the question. He had assumed he was probably the last person left in the area, in this little corner of the world, but depending on where she had come from it was astoundingly bad news. He had tried his best to remain at least somewhat hopeful, had worked hard to convince himself that he couldn't be the last person left in the world. That apparently wasn't true, not completely, since he was looking at Krissy right in front of him, but it was still fairly disheartening. "How far have you traveled?"

Krissy paused to take a swig from the bottle of water in her pack, doing the calculations in her head as she screwed the lid back on. "Oh, probably thirty or forty miles since I first took off. I decided to avoid the highway, I figured there would be a lot of accidents all over and if there were any looters or people like that still around there wouldn't really be any good places to hide out there. So I went with the back roads, veering off now and then to check out places that seemed like they might be worthwhile. I spent weeks just sleeping in houses along the way, trying to find ones that didn't have any dead inside which was harder than I wanted to believe it would be.

"I ended up out by the caves and I followed that road pretty far, then when I started running low on provisions I decided to head out this way. I was going to go on into town, but decided to try out here first. I was just doing the same thing as before, finding empty houses and bunking down for a day or two to rest before moving on. It feels like I've been doing this forever, just moving on and on and finding nothing. It was so strange too, how many places were pretty emptied out. I guess people who ended up sick had been using up their little stockpiles until it happened, and then some of the people who took off before that happened packed up just about everything they could take. What about you? How has it been out here?"

Avery debated internally on how much to tell her, getting up from his seat and going to his pile of extra blankets. He got her one and handed it over, watching as she shed her winter coat and wrapped the dry material around her instead. She was pretty thin, and she had dark circles under her eyes that were likely due to lack of sleep. He could imagine why. It would have been awful just always being on the go and finding shelter anywhere you could, and it made him feel a little bit more like her story was checking out.

"Sort of the same, but maybe not nearly as bad. We had a good storage of food over last winter, and it was just starting to run low when I ended up alone. I salvaged everything that was left and then moved in over here, and then I really started foraging and hoarding up supplies. I hit all the nearby houses and some a few miles out, getting whatever could be saved and used. Then I hit the grocery store in town, but I didn't wipe it clean right away. I went back a few times for things as I ran low, but it's finally out of everything that's still edible," he explained to her, dropping back down onto the mattress with Tilly by his side. "I got some useful stuff from the hardware store and the pharmacy, and I even went into a few houses in town. Some had a few things left, but most just weren't worth it."

For him it felt like grave robbing still, which is how he had tried to explain it to his mother all those months ago. He only took what he thought he truly needed for survival, which was primarily canned goods, and there were some things he wouldn't take from a house with the dead still inside. Blankets and other gear he took from houses that had been abandoned, the owners long gone and not coming back. It made him feel a little bit less like he was doing something explicitly wrong, removing the horrible nature of it from his conscious.

Krissy seemed impressed by the fact that he had created a good stockpile of goods and other supplies, glancing around at the shadowy shelves and cubbies full of just about everything a person could need. Nails, screws, several kinds of glue, paper, pens, the blow torch he'd used to break into the pharmacy. Everything had a potential use, a purpose or a re-purpose, and he was taking absolutely nothing for granted.

"Your dog doesn't like me," she finally said, looking at the beagle who was staring right back at her from her spot beside Avery on the bed. "Does she bite?"

"If she was going to bite you she would have already," Avery pointed out with another shrug. "She hasn't seen another living soul but me in months now, and she didn't trust most people to begin with anyway. She might warm up to you, but she might not either. I'd just avoid putting my hands anywhere near her face until she decides."

"Noted," Krissy agreed, shifting a little and looking away from the dog finally. "We can't turn the heat up? It's warmer than outside but just barely. I had a fireplace in the cabin, and the people who lived there before had a whole cord of wood out back. It was nice, so much so that I nearly considered just staying and trying to make my rations last. At least then I wouldn't have been hungry and cold, just hungry."

Avery looked uneasy at the idea, still planning to make the gas stretch as long as he could. This was only December, and they had to last until at least March. The coldest months were still up ahead, and he found himself finally shaking his head. "No, I have to conserve the gas. When the temperature really starts to plummet in January we'll be using more of it, and I don't want to risk running out before then since I don't know how much is actually in the tank. I think it was pretty full, but I don't know that for certain."

Krissy was poised to argue but then changed her mind, knowing she had no real place to do so. This guy was letting her stay here for at least the night, though she did catch the use of the word we'll, which implied he was going to maybe let her stay longer. Either that or he was regarding the dog in all of his statements, which was certainly possible. People had always been gaga over their pets, and why should an apocalyptic plague change that?

"Fair enough," she told him finally, pulling the blanket a little tighter around herself. "I don't want you going out of your way, I did just randomly appear at your door and I'm lucky you even let me in. So I'm already feeling pretty thankful, truth be told."

"Getting through the winter is the hardest part about all of this. It's a harsh time even under good circumstances, but now the odds are stacked against us and we have to just be super careful. It's all about survival, about getting to the other side, and I try to just keep focused on that," he told her, getting up again to go back to the pile of blankets. "Why don't you tell me your story though, I'm interested. I only know my own experiences; it would be nice to hear about someone else for a change. You up for that?"

"I think I can be," Krissy answered slowly, a little unsure about hashing it all out but willing to do so if he asked. Both of them had been starved for human interaction for a long time now, and it wasn't as though they had anything better to do with their time. It was dark and the storm was raging, and they had heat and company so there was really no time like the present. "I'm from Glendale, just down the highway, so I guess we should start there…"

FOURTEEN

"I'M FROM GLENDALE, JUST DOWN THE HIGHWAY, so I guess we should start there," Krissy told him, a faraway sort of look in her eyes as she leaned back against the bank of post boxes and began her story. "It was pretty much the same as it was in most places in the beginning; we all thought something like that would never spread our way. It was ravaging mostly big cities after those first people got sick in Louisiana, all it took was one person coughing on public transit and boom! Suddenly it was sweeping through Atlanta, then Savannah, and up the coast to Charleston. It just kept going, spreading all over the place from sick people on airplanes or people who had come down with it already and were trying to flee before they started showing symptoms. Those places were so far from here, so far from us, and even when it hit Louisville and then Lexington it still wasn't enough to scare everyone."

It sounded a lot like what Avery had experienced, which stood to reason. Glendale was just a few miles down the highway, and it made sense that they had thought in a similar fashion. While they weren't exactly as rural as Graven, located slap in the middle of nowhere, it still wasn't a place with a lot of action going on. It all felt so stupid now though, how safe so many people had felt because of their geographical location. In the end that had mattered not one whit.

While Krissy talked Avery did get up and went back into the front, getting the leftover soup that he hadn't finished from earlier in the day. He turned on the small camp stove and got out his cooking pot, starting to heat it up for her. If she was willing to share about herself and be open with him, the least he could do was give her something hot to eat in exchange.

"Go on," he encouraged her, eager to hear someone else's story to see how it differed from his own. "What happened when people started getting sick?"

Krissy paid close attention to what he was doing, her stomach growling despite the candy bar she had eaten. "Bedlam," she told him, tugging at the blanket around her shoulders where it had started to slip. "After the first confirmed case it was like people were still in disbelief, just totally unwilling to accept it. Then it started spreading through the staff of the clinic where a lady had gone when she'd first started feeling sick, and then it spread a little bit more. People started to panic, trying to get out of town as fast as they could. I lived in a quiet neighborhood on a side street near the courthouse, and we all agreed to work together to help one another. That turned out to not be the best idea in the world."

Avery handed her a steaming bowl of soup and she sipped at it without bothering to use a spoon. It was still too hot so she just held it in her hands, staring at him across the grate on the floor as he settled back onto the air bed. She continued her story, steam rising from the bowl as she waited for it to cool enough to not burn her tongue off.

"An elderly man down the block got sick first, and we all tried to help his wife. We took some provisions, clean water, extra blankets, but he only lasted three days before he died. She came down with it next, and then one of the women who had jumped in to help started coughing. We realized then that we weren't going to be able to help in that way, so we tried other things. We all did a community food source, just the people on my street, sharing our food and fresh water. That went downhill quickly too, some people were greedier than others, so we started storing our own stuff in a locked cabinet. Then my aunt, I lived with her, got sick. She told me to stay away, and I did. I didn't want to risk getting sick myself, and two days later she was gone and I was alone."

That sounded familiar too, and it made Avery frown hard. Every single person had been touched by tragedy early on in the course of the Ruger Virus, and they were the only two people who now had to continue living with their losses. It hurt immeasurably, and he felt for her in that moment. He had lost a sister, a father, and a mother over the course of a year, but she had felt the loss too and he knew that no one person's grief was more important than the next person's. That, at least, was one part of humanity they were still able to cling onto tightly.

"I'm sorry about your aunt," Avery told her then, his words very sincere. "I know what that's like. I lost my family too, which is part of how I ended up here. That was the worst part, I think, having that happen. It's worse than just being alone, and it's how we ended up like this at all that hurts more than anything else."

Krissy nodded in agreement, the bowl tipped again as she took a swallow. It was canned vegetable soup, salty but hearty, and she had to force herself to pause for a breath. She wiped her mouth with the back of her hand, manners a thing of the past in some regards. "Yeah, that got me," she self-confessed, tapping her thumbs against the rim of the bowl as she gave her stomach a second to settle. "I ended up next door with our neighbors, the Cooke's, who had two little kids. I brought what food and things I had with me, but they were already running low when I showed up. Didn't take long for that situation to go south either."

Another pause to finish off the bowl of soup, sitting it aside with a satisfied sigh as she rested her hands across her now full and warm stomach. She looked up toward the ceiling then, as though staring at a fixed point, and Avery got the idea that she was probably trying not to cry. He didn't blame her for that; nobody wanted to appear weak in front of a total stranger at the end of the world.

"Food was starting to get scarce, and things were falling apart in town. Business owners had more or less locked up and said see ya later, even the places that had plenty of food on hand like restaurants and grocery stores. I figure that a lot of the owners and managers probably took whatever they could use when they closed up shop, but some people weren't taking no for an answer," she said, wrinkling her nose up a little bit in disgust. "They started looting, just busting out windows and breaking down doors. They took everything they could carry from the places that had stuff worth taking, and they weren't interested in sharing. It never made the news, because why would it? People were dropping dead by the thousands, a food shortage in Glendale, Kentucky wasn't going to be worthwhile."

Her tone was bitter when she said that, shaking her head and getting another small sip of water from the big bottle she had on hand. She offered a drink to Avery who merely shook his head and gestured for her to continue. "The dad, Roger Cooke, said we had to have something to eat and he wasn't going to let his kids starve. He took off on a Wednesday, and that was the last time we saw anything of him. We don't know if he got sick while he was out and tried to hole up somewhere, or if he got caught up in the mess going on and someone took him out. Either way he was out of the picture, and there were four of us who still had to make it. The mom got sick not long after and died in the upstairs bathroom, and I was left trying to take care of two little kids. We ate crab apples and stale crackers for days until I saw the people across the street loading up their cars and leaving. I was able to get into their house and take everything they hadn't bothered to pack up. There was a lot of frozen stuff, but there was still power and everything then so it worked out."

Avery thought about him and his mother, about how the neighbors had all sort of fled at once to try and escape the sickness. They couldn't outrun it, so it likely had caught up with them not far out, but their departure had at least been some gain. The things they had left behind had been beneficial to the survival of those that stayed, and those were the houses he didn't feel one little bit bad about robbing blind.

"The kids, Tommy and Ricky, were okay for a little while. We lasted about a month there in their parents' house," Krissy continued, rubbing the end of her nose out of nervous habit.

"They were four and six, too little to be much help, and Tommy got sick with it first. Ricky died two days after his brother, and that was it. I was the last one standing, and I knew something had to change. I packed up what I could find and I started walking. I knew how dire things really were when I went across the overpass and got a real look at the interstate. Just cars as far as you could see in both directions, overturned big rigs, doors open on vehicles where people just abandoned them and tried to flee on foot. It was like something out of a movie or comic book, and I made the decision to follow the back roads right then and there. There was just something eerie about it, something wrong, and I formulated a plan and I stuck with it."

Avery listened intently as Krissy recounted how she had walked for a few miles that day, ending up in a church that you could see from the highway. She had taken up refuge there, spending a day and a night sleeping on a stiff pew to get some of her energy back. She had taken the snacks from the Sunday school rooms and put them into her pack before moving on, figuring gummy candies and goldfish crackers were better than nothing. She'd kept to the main road for a little while and then veered off, trying side roads and hollers in an attempt to find someone else who was alive and trying to get by. She took what she could find from empty houses as she went along, though she tried to avoid the places with the dead inside. The smell was always a giveaway, and she designated those places as not being worth it.

It had taken her a couple of weeks to reach the road that went out toward the caves, and she tried there too. The cabin she had found was off a narrow, winding side road with sharp curves and not a lot of houses. By that point it was getting chilly, and she had gathered up enough stuff to justify laying low for a while. The cabin was small and rustic, probably used for hunting or just on weekends as he had suspected, but that was a great benefit to her. It was easy to heat using the pot belly wood stove, and it was easy for cooking on too. She kept the fire stoked all of the time, only going out when she felt it was necessary to bring in more wood or to just stretch her legs.

"More than anything else, I felt lonely," Krissy told him, rubbing her nose again and sighing softly. "I've never liked being alone, and that was a driving force too in me leaving the cabin and heading this way. I was running low on food, yes, but most of all I was still so desperate to just find someone else. I wanted someone to talk to, someone to work on getting by with. Survival is so much harder when you're on your own, and I really don't know how you've done so well."

"I had no other choice, and it was do or die," Avery answered her simply, scratching Tilly on top of the head as he settled back into the middle of the mattress. "I had to have food, so I found it. I needed other supplies, so I got them. I worked all through the late summer and fall to put all this together, to make sure I had a shot at getting through the winter. Anyway once it's over I plan to move on, to find somewhere better to go. That's my next big step, and I just have to wait for the weather to turn fair again. The last thing I want to do is get stuck somewhere without a place to stay or anything. The snow falls pretty deep in some places too, it'll make the roads less passable. I need conditions to be as good as they can be."

Krissy looked very interested in his idea, leaning forward a little bit so the warm air from the grate hit her right in the face and made her blink her eyes a little faster. "The back roads aren't so awful, it's just the highways and in town that things are a mess. You can probably make it pretty far before you hit any real, impassable obstacles. Where do you think you might go? Have you thought that far ahead or are you just in the planning stages? At least you have a plan beyond just hoping to stumble upon someone else. In retrospect it wasn't the brightest idea I ever had, and it could have ended pretty badly."

"No idea yet," Avery said, grabbing the atlas. He held it up to show it to her, feeling a bit sheepish now. "I've started looking at different possibilities, marking off different routes, and trying to calculate what it would take to get there. I have to consider food and fuel and all that stuff, and probably will end up having to change vehicles along the way. It would be easier to just move what I'm taking from one car to another and not have to deal with moving the fuel from one to the other."

"Let me see," Krissy told him rather than asked, leaning across further to snag the edge of the atlas. She plucked it from his hands before he had the chance to protest, flipping through the pages and eyeballing the things he had marked and noted. "These are all south. You want to be somewhere warmer, clearly. Why not north? I mean there might be a better chance of running into other people if you go north. What about like Washington? There has to be people left there, you know they didn't risk the whole government just dying out."

Avery made a face at the mention of traveling any further north, shaking his head adamantly. "No way! Look, I'm not interested in finding a big group of politicians who have no fix for any of this. What are they going to do? They aren't any better off than the rest of us these days except they're probably eating steaks in whatever bunker they're holed up in. No, south is the only way. It's warmer down there, has better year-round weather. I'm not far enough south here, and Tennessee wouldn't cut it either. It has to be somewhere that has a more temperate climate, somewhere that you can grow food all year long. In a place like that I could cultivate a lot of my own food without worrying about scavenging. Canned goods won't last forever either, there's a finite amount and they'll either go off and be bad for you to eat, or won't be left at all after a certain point anyway. We can't rely on stuff like that to keep sustaining us, because the world could take a long time to heal and repair if it ever does.

"This was global; it had spread off the continent well before the news broadcasts cut out. Humanity might well be over after this, this could be the catastrophe everyone was always sort of just waiting for. Maybe it spread faster because of global warming, maybe it's God punishing us for our sins, I don't know what it is. I only know that we can't be dependent on what was man made for much longer, and we're going to have to think outside the box. I'd rather be down there knowing I might have to contend with a hurricane or something than to live somewhere that made me struggle six months of the year. I mean we're different people, we just met each other, and we each have our own ideas. If you want to go north, by all means go north. I, however, am taking Tilly and going south where I stand a better chance."

Krissy looked like she very much wanted to argue, but instead she just let her shoulders fall in a sort of resigned way and nodded her head in agreement. "Okay, okay. I've got the point, and I'm sorry for suggesting that your plan was wrong somehow. Let's not be hasty either though, because we did just meet each other and maybe this is something that can be good for both of us. I mean two people are more efficient at things than just one person, right? I'd like to at least maybe have the option to move on with you somewhere better once spring comes. If we end up hating each other or something, though, at least we know we're comfortable going our separate ways."

It was strange to Avery that Krissy would already be considering following him once spring came. That implied that she was also hoping to be here with him when the seasons changed. It didn't really bother him necessarily, it was nice to have the company of another living person, but something just felt amiss. He knew that things like trust took time to build, and he wanted to get to the point of trusting her, but he had to let it happen naturally. He couldn't force it, especially not after meeting her under such unusual circumstances, but he had confidence that they could get there.

"I am sorry if I bothered you at all by disagreeing," Krissy apologized, feeling the need to keep trying to explain herself and what she had said. He figured she was probably afraid he'd tell her she had to go, which was ludicrous though she didn't know that it was. There were a lot of people in the world, or at least before in the world, who hadn't been able to tolerate dissent of any kind very well. "I just thought there might be people in Washington or somewhere who could help us, who might have some sort of safe zone for survivors. Probably I've just been watching too much prime time television and all that. Your idea is a good one, to go somewhere that you can set up a sustainable lifestyle without having to constantly be battling the seasons. You have a bunch of routes set up to Louisiana. Is that your primary contender?"

"One of them," Avery nodded, taking back the atlas from her so he could look at his own scribbled notes. "The weather there would be nice, and there should be some good places for farming. It's pretty far though, and not entirely practical. Georgia wouldn't be so bad either, maybe somewhere nearer to the coast. I wish so bad that I could get hold of some good books, to try and learn more about all these places and if they would be as good of options as they are in my mind. It's too late though, the weather isn't good enough to risk a run into town to try and get into the library. I was there once before, and I should have thought about it then but I didn't, which is just bad planning on my part."

Krissy pursed her lips in thought and they were quiet for a stretch of time, both of them just lost in their own thoughts. Finally she yawned and rubbed at her eyes, laughing a little as her vision blurred from sleepiness. "Is it okay if I crash? I'll try to stay out of your way," she told him, offering him back the blanket.

"Keep it, I have more," he told her as he got to his feet, grabbing her one of the two pillows from his bed and some more of the blankets from his stack. "Here, you can make yourself a little nest. I don't have another air bed, so hopefully the floor isn't too hard or cold for you. You can sleep up close to the grate though on that other side and I think it'll keep you plenty warm enough. I'll turn it back off in the morning and back on again tomorrow night if it stays this cold."

"You're a very meticulous person," she complimented him, taking the offered bed linens and starting to make the aforementioned nest on the floor. She layered up the blankets to try and make the floor more bearable; folding her coat up to use as a second pillow since the first wasn't very thick. She wrapped up in two more blankets and then laid down, curling herself up into a ball. "Thank you for this, Avery, really. I don't know what I would have ended up doing if I hadn't found you. You didn't have to let me in but you did, and that means more than you can imagine."

Avery gave her a smile and a nod in return, turning the lamp down until the light went out. He lay in the shadows for a good long while, listening until her breathing grew deeper and more even. Once he was sure she was out he climbed carefully from his own bed, flicking on the small pen light to help him see in the dark room. He found the shotgun and he hid it away in a space between the counter and the wall, stowing the bullets on top of the bank of mailboxes where she couldn't reach or see them. He also got his hunting knife and slipped it carefully into the bottom of his pillowcase, figuring he needed to take some precautions.

No matter what she said or the circumstances they had found themselves in, Krissy was still very much a stranger and he didn't trust her. Not totally, anyway, though he did feel sorry for her to a degree. She had stumbled upon him somehow, some way, and didn't seem to have much of anything. That part of the story probably checked out okay, but what about the rest? He didn't find any glaring holes in what she had told him, but something still felt off. Likely it was just unease from being alone for so long, with nobody around and certainly not anybody else here in this little safe haven he had cultivated for himself. Krissy was an interloper, and he had to tread carefully until he knew better.

With the gun hidden and his knife close by, Avery climbed back onto the air mattress and put the flashlight down near his head. Tilly did her usual three turns and curled up against his legs under the blankets, the air coming from the grate helping to keep them that much warmer which was becoming increasingly necessary at night as they got deeper into winter. He laid on his side facing Krissy, watching for movement as he slowly drifted off. He knew it wouldn't be a good sleep, not even close to peaceful, but he had gotten something he had been thinking about for a long time.

There was someone else alive. He wasn't the only survivor.

FIFTEEN

THE SNOW STORM DIED OUT THE MORNING AFTER Krissy Rawlins arrived at Avery's hideout, but they stayed primarily indoors until it warmed up enough to melt off the lingering snow. They ventured out beneath the makeshift shelter to get a fire going, Avery in his lawn chair and Krissy perching on an empty mail tote she had found. They warmed up and cooked food there, melting snow down into fresh water. As it began to boil in the pot, Avery began to lay plans to do one more sweep of the neighborhood, hoping to find some leftovers he might have missed during his previous visits. It was rare he'd gone into a house twice, but it felt like it was time.

After all it seemed as though Krissy was intending to stay, and he didn't have the heart to kick her out even though he still felt unsure about her. Two people meant twice as many provisions as far as food went, and he wanted to get a handle on things before it snowed again.

As soon as the snowdrifts turned to puddles he was ready, grabbing his bag before he told her the plan. He had initially intended to go alone, but Krissy was going a bit stir crazy too and elected to come along. A person could only spend so much time indoors, eating small portions of canned food and reading books. Avery saw no real reason why she shouldn't accompany him, and so they set out with Tilly to see what they could possibly find.

"I'd never been over this way before," Krissy acknowledged as they headed up the road, going past the bridge and starting the uphill trek. There were houses all along the ridge, and a few of them Avery hadn't visited at all before. He knew it would likely require going in where there were dead folks, but that was just something they would have to do. He hated it, but he hated the idea of starving to death worse. "I never even really knew what was out here. Was Graven a real town at some point?"

Avery cast a sideways glance at her and then shook his head, walking with his back stooped a little as they trudged along the sharp incline and into the curve. "No, not really, but I guess it depends on how you define a town. It's just always been an unincorporated blip in the middle of nowhere really, and I guess the brickyard was its claim to fame. It was running until right up before the virus got set loose, which is probably for the better. There were a lot of people in and out of there every day, truck drivers and workers, and it might have spread even faster with those folks around. We just had that and the post office, and years ago there were more company buildings and the school. It closed up a long time ago though, when most of the other stuff did. It's not much and never was, but it's always been home."

Krissy listened as they walked, a little out of breath by the time they crested the hill and came out at the top of the ridge. She had walked this once already, and she didn't like it anymore now than she had a few days ago. "There's a lot of houses, must have been quite a few people. It's sad that this happened and that it even got into these small places. Makes me wonder how much is left out there."

"I'm sad to leave; I've never lived anywhere else. I know it's necessary though, and I'll be glad to get to a place where I can be more stable. I hope there are others, and I hope we run into them at some point. It makes me feel like there's hope to imagine this isn't it," Avery answered, turning onto a road that branched off to the left.

The first house was one he hadn't touched yet, a big a-frame log home with a sloped red tin roof and three vehicles outside. The place was quiet, and it gave him a bad feeling, but going into untouched places was the most logical move to make before he started repeating old patterns. He started up the driveway, peering into the cars but seeing nothing of interest. Krissy followed him up the steps and onto the covered porch, where he tried the knob and found the door locked. He searched around since he had forgotten to bring his crowbar, spotting a decorative flower pot sitting on the porch rail. He used that to break the window out, reaching inside to undo the two locks and shove the door open.

"Lack of alarm systems has certainly made it easier to break and enter," Avery joked, though he didn't even really crack a smile as he said it. He knew there were people who would have taken advantage of situations like this, though they would never get a chance. That was a weird sort of blessing and curse, and it made him feel awful to consider it. "Not that I was practiced in the art of breaking and entering before this, so please don't think I'm a professional. All skills were developed clumsily after Ruger came."

"Got it," Krissy smiled, stepping into the house with him. There was a lingering sweet smell, sickly and strong, and she pulled her coat up to cover her nose and mouth. The smell didn't bother Avery nearly as much; he had smelled far worse, though he did hope they wouldn't stumble onto the homes previous residents.

They had entered a living room with tall windows that were tinted a bit to cut some of the glare. They crept through the room quietly, Tilly sniffing along the dusty wood floors as they moved. The living room opened right up into a roomy kitchen, with lots of cabinets and a door that opened into a vast pantry. The pair of them worked wordlessly then, Krissy going into the pantry with a flashlight while Avery began to open cabinets.

Luck was with them on that first stop, the cabinets holding several canned goods with some of them still in date. He took everything that was still good and a few things, like a jar of peanut butter, which he thought might still be okay. He put them into the duffel and then checked on Krissy, pleased to see she had found some boxes of pasta noodles, a jar of in-date sauce, and some packages of Oreo cookies that had likely been intended for a lunch box. They added it all into the bag and he threw it back over his shoulder, shuffling back through the living room.

They worked like that for the better part of an hour, trying some more homes that Avery hadn't been inside of yet with mixed results. They found one or two items in some places, and nothing at all in others. The fifth house they went in had been an immediate no-go, a dead man sprawled across the living room sofa when they had entered. There was a blanket partially draped over top of him, and he was in a serious state of decomposition. The smell alone had been overwhelming, and Avery had waited patiently by the road while Krissy stepped into the woods to throw up.

After that the mood for exploration began to dwindle, and they instead went back to some of the places that Avery had previously visited. He led her into a house trailer first, heading straight to the kitchen with a purpose. He began to open all the cabinets for a secondary check, speaking over his shoulder as he worked.

"Terry Ames lived here," he told her, a hint of sadness to his voice. "He was a good guy, he used to have a farm, but he lost it to the bank when he lost his job at the brickyard. His brother owned this place and let him move in to help him out. He did some odd jobs for my dad, sometimes helped him with big deliveries in the truck. It wasn't much, but he was always willing to do what he could for people and so people wanted to do good for him too. He got sick pretty early on and his niece took him to UK to the hospital. He died before they even got him admitted; right in the emergency room is what everyone said. That's what I hate most about the Ruger Virus, you know? It didn't discriminate, it just killed everybody. Good people, bad people, it didn't know the difference, so it just took them all. Except us, we were the lucky ones. Or the unlucky who got left behind, depending on how you look at it."

All they found in Terry Ames abandoned home was a solitary can of deviled ham that Avery had missed the first time around. They took it and then left, careful to lock and shut the door behind them. Avery knew that locking the door was just symbolic, it didn't mean anything anymore, but it felt good to do it and it signified that this was his last visit. He wouldn't be back here again, and it was likely that nobody else would ever be either.

Neither of them felt much like continuing the search, and he was fine with that. They'd gotten some good spoils, and a little bit could go a long way if they made it stretch. They started their trek back down the hill, and this time as they walked, Avery told her more about Graven. He told her about the brickyard and how they had supplied the building boom after the Second World War and beyond. His great-grandfather and grandfather had worked there, and so had his father for a time driving the truck that carried the raw materials in and the fire bricks back out. He had never had any ambitions to be part of the masses who had dedicated their blood, sweat, and tears to the brickyard, but he supposed that he might have had it stayed open.

Had it stayed open, and if the Ruger Virus hadnot taken everything else that was left. It made him feel mad all over again, and he could have screamed his head off. He thought about it anyway, but he didn't want to come off as being some sort of psycho. He settled instead for keeping his lips pursed together, staring at his feet as they reached the bottom of the hill.

"Where did you live?" Krissy asked then, as they stood at the junction that led either up the hill, across the bridge, or to the post office. "I know you said it was gone and everything, but I'm just curious. You can tell me to shut up though if you want, I won't be offended at all."

"Give me a minute," Avery said, voice a bit more gruff than before. He left her there and took the bag into the post office, dropping it into the backroom before he rejoined her. Tilly ran ahead of them, chasing after a red bird that had been lit on a low tree branch.

Together they crossed the bridge and turned right, walking past the sprawling old school building. He told her that he had first thought about making that his new residence but had abandoned the idea when he had considered how drafty and cold it would likely be in the winter months. There were a lot of windows and no gas heating system anymore, everything running on electricity. He'd have had to get enough propane and kerosene to last, and it would have been a lot more trouble than it would have been worth. Plus, he didn't need all that room, it would have felt strange and haunted, so in the end the post office had been the best choice for him.

Beyond the school the hillside opened up, dotted with small houses. There were steps leading from the road up to the homes that remained, but he led her to a place where a small driveway curved up to a now empty flat spot. He gestured to it, and after looking a bit closer Krissy realized there were the charred remnants of a house, only the foundation and ash now remaining.

"My little sister, Jessa, she died first," he whispered, head tilted back a little to stare up at the cloudless winter sky. "She just got sick all of a sudden, and we figured it might have been in the well water. She died fast, and we all thought that we'd come down with it too. We called that phone number, the one from the CDC, and they came to take her body. They locked us all up in there and we had to wait it out with the germs. We made it somehow though, and that was when people just started to up and leave. My dad lost it though, something in him snapped, and he decided he couldn't just wait to get sick and die. He killed himself in the living room after me and my mom went to bed."

Avery moved over to the cold concrete steps of the house next door and sat down; sighing as he pulled his knees up and rested his arms across them. He didn't look at Krissy as he kept talking, just lost inside of his own memories for the moment. "We were starting to run low on food, so mom went into that house right down there, the one with the wrought iron porch railing. The people inside had just died, and I guess she contracted it from there. Like maybe they hadn't been dead long enough or maybe the germs had just been sort of stewing. She drank some water she found in their fridge too, so maybe it really was in the water. Anyway, she died in our house here, in the upstairs bedroom, and I knew I had to leave then. I couldn't stay there after my whole family died inside, so I set it on fire with her body still inside and I left."

It was incredibly weird to be telling this story to someone else after holding it inside for months. He hadn't anticipated ever telling it, and he almost wished that he hadn't. That was a little silly, it wasn't like he hadn't done the right thing or had done something incredibly awful, but it still made him feel strange inside. Like maybe he could have done something differently or tried harder in some way. What could he have done though? His mother had gotten sick, just like Jessa, and his father had been an adult man capable of his own choices. Everything that had happened would have happened no matter what, and he knew he had to let those feelings of inadequacy go.

"I'm sorry," Krissy said softly after a while, reaching over to touch the back of his hand gently with her fingers. "Losing a family member is awful, that's for sure. We all want to turn back the clock and do things over, but this was out of our control. It always was, and no matter how many times we went back to try and change it, the outcome would probably just always be the same. I miss my mom too though, that's for sure."

Avery thought back to when Krissy had told him her story a few days previous, but she hadn't mentioned her parents then. She'd mentioned the aunt she lived with, but not a single word about a mother or father. She had them, of course, in some capacity but it felt like a bizarre disconnect. She was speaking as though she had lost her mother in a similar way but had been living with her aunt when the Ruger Virus had broken out. Or was he simply mistaken? Maybe she had been initially living with her parents and came to the aunts when they had fallen ill. He didn't think he'd misconstrued her words so badly, but he wouldn't rule it out as being impossible just yet.

Instead of trying to accuse her though and making things weird he merely nodded, pulling himself slowly back to his feet. His joints ached a bit, too many nights on the air mattress he figured, stretching a little so things popped and gave him some relief. He held out a hand to help her up, shuffling his feet as they started to walk again.

"I miss everyone, a lot. I even miss my sister, who practically lived to drive me up the wall. She could be a pretty fun kid too, and we had a lot of good times. Just watching movies or helping mom around the house. We weren't siblings who were best friends, but we were close enough and probably would have gotten closer when she got older," he expressed, kicking at some rocks as they ventured back across the bridge to get back to the post office.

"I miss my dad all the time, he was a pretty serious guy. He taught me a lot of useful skills though, but not nearly enough. I had a lot left to learn, and it bothers me that I'll never get to have him teach me. Mom I miss most of all, she was the best. She kept us all together, she was the glue, and she had a good outlook on everything. Just one mistake though and that was it, all snuffed out, and it wasn't fair at all. I'll never understand why I lived, and she didn't, but I guess I shouldn't question something I'll never have the answer to."

Krissy rubbed her gloved hands together as they got back to the office, heading in through the back door. It was time for dinner, which meant getting the matches to build the fire back up, and then selecting what they'd throw together today. "You might get an answer someday," she told him then, getting out one of the boxes of pasta that they'd just found. It sounded good after all sorts of soup and tuna, getting a pot to fill with the last remnants of snow outside. "Maybe you're immune and maybe I am too. Maybe eventually some scientists hiding in a bunker somewhere will crawl back out and go on the hunt for survivors. Maybe we'll know the answers sooner rather than later."

Avery stepped outside the door to put wood in the fire pit, snorting a little as he looked back at her. "You've clearly watched too many movies," he quipped, striking a match and bringing into the kindling. "Nothing is going to happen but this right here, just in a different place maybe. Once you accept that? Things will be a hell of a lot better for you, believe me."

SIXTEEN

DESPITE THE UNCERTAINTY THAT HE WAS FEELING, Avery allowed Krissy to continue to stay through the winter. The weather fluctuated, as Kentucky weather was wont to do, some days cold and snowy while others were impossibly warm. Most of their time was spent in the shelter they were now sharing, though some clear and sunny days were spent doing nearby runs for provisions. When Tilly finally ran out of dog food they were suddenly splitting rations three ways, which was not something he had ever anticipated happening. By late February they were running low enough that he felt worried, pacing the creaking floorboards as rain poured down outside. The soggy, wet weather was even worse than the snow, with the rain keeping them from even getting the fire going again even with his makeshift lean-to. That meant either eating cold food or using the camp stove, and both options had him feeling cranky.

"We have to do something else," he complained, kicking an

empty soup can across the room where it banged off the wall in an only somewhat satisfactory way. "Maybe we need to venture further out, try some places I haven't thought about before. February is a bad month, we usually get a big snowstorm, and then we have to have stuff to take when we leave. By the time we get to that point everything will be gone, we'll be totally screwed!"

Krissy sat on her nest of blankets, watching him walk the floor. He went back and forth from the front counter to the back windows, the rain pounding onto the roof overhead. Tilly lay beside of her just out of reach, warmed up to the girl a little but not enough to want to be too close. Together they just stared at him, listening to his rant until it faded into silence. At first she didn't know what to say or how to answer him, finally shrugging her shoulders and biting her bottom lip.

"There has to be something left out there, or something we haven't tried yet. You have a gun, right? Have you tried hunting? I mean you do have a dog," she pointed out, though she almost recoiled at the look he gave her. She didn't particularly care for these moods he had been having lately, wishing she could do more to squelch out his nerves. "Maybe you're right, maybe on the next sunny day we just go out a little further. There are a lot of big houses out toward the caves that I never went into, those may be pretty well stocked still."

Avery wasn't especially fond of having to keep searching, of having to go further away than he had been since the whole thing had started, but they had to do something. He finally stopped pacing and sighed, running his hands through his hair. "I was never really into the whole hunting thing, even though my dad was. I went a few times as a kid, but during bow season because he didn't trust me yet with a gun. I can shoot it, but it kicks bad and I've mostly kept it for protection. You know, if someone unsavory showed up it might be enough to scare them off. I don't want to waste the shells either, because we might need them. Especially when we're on the road, I want the security of it."

Krissy nodded a little, and though she didn't fully understand she could at least grasp a bit of where he was coming from. "Gotcha. Okay, so, we just try and find enough to get through the last bit of winter, and then we focus on packing up for the trip. You have to remember that we can always stop and forage along the way too, this isn't the only place we can get food and supplies. We'll pass through towns, cities, and everything in between going wherever we ultimately choose to go. Don't let yourself think about that too much yet, alright?"

"There's gas left in the Camaro," Avery told her then, dropping down to sit on the floor where he had been standing. He pulled his long legs in and crossed them, chewing on the corner of his thumbnail as he thought. "Definitely enough to get us out to the place you're talking about and back, a good little day trip. If we can just get enough to get by, that will be alright for now. You're right about one thing, that I don't need to focus too much on the trip. I just need to focus on right now."

Krissy gave him a smile then, mostly relieved that he seemed to be calming down. She gave him a nod of encouragement too, clapping her hands together in a pleased way. "Yes! So the next nice day we have we just go. We get your duffel bag and Tilly and we load up. It's not too far, and we can make a full day of it if we try so we aren't wasting gas or our time either. We may even be able to find enough to have a surplus started for when we leave. We just have to think positive!"

Avery snorted out a laugh and then laid back, unfurling his legs as he stretched out. Tilly rose from her spot and came over to lick his face, and he rewarded her by ruffling and scratching at her floppy beagle ears. He was not the most optimistic person, which was why he had been so meticulous and arduous with his planning and stockpiling. It drove him a little crazy too that all his careful work had been undone by unforeseen circumstances, but such was life. Nothing went according to the initial plan, not even after the apocalypse seemed to have come, but that was just something he had to learn to deal with.

The next nice day came two days after the rainstorm, when the rain stopped, and the rising creek waters receded enough for him to consider them less of a threat. Just as Krissy had said they loaded up the duffel bag and Tilly and set off in the Camaro with Avery at the wheel. The day was warm so they rolled the windows down since both of them were sweating inside flannel shirts, the radio blaring a cd of classic rock music as they flew along the winding backroads.

Once they hit the main road though Avery exercised more caution, especially near the exit ramps on and off the interstate. Both of them were jammed with abandoned cars, a few of them still sitting out in the road where they hadn't been able to go any further. He carefully navigated between a tow truck and an old church van, heading out toward the caves well below the speed limit. It wasn't a long drive but it seemed to take a small eternity for them to reach the first house. It was on the right side of the main road, near the entrance to the state park but not quite inside of it. It was a big place with a rock façade and lots of white trim, a huge window in the front showing a glimpse of what was inside. From the road you could only see peeks of a sofa and a television through the partially drawn curtains, but it was as good of a place to start as any.

    They were able to enter through the unlocked garage door, which opened up right into the kitchen. The place was quiet and smelled musty, without a lingering scent of death in the air. There had been no vehicles in the garage or the driveway, so Avery figured the people had likely fled the coop ages ago when the getting out had been supposedly good. It seemed too that they had taken all the nonperishable items with them, since the only things left were long spoiled. Rotten fruit so mushy and brown they couldn't tell apples from oranges, and loaves of bread molded green in the packages. It was certainly disappointing, and a quick sweep of the other rooms told a similar tale. They had left things like the television and big pieces of furniture, but other things were noticeably missing. There were no family portraits on the walls, and blank spots on the bookshelves whre items had been removed. They had taken the time to pack important items with them, obviously not anticipating ever coming back.

    After the letdown of the first house they headed straight for the road to the caves, where the houses were large and very expensive. There were some spoils to be found, including a house that had entirely too much canned meat in the cupboards. They found everything from canned salmon to canned chicken, and even some tinned gravy that was still well within date. Avery made sure to get all of that, because the only way he thought he could eat canned chicken was to cover it in enough gravy to mask the metallic taste of it. No matter what though it was food, and they couldn't really afford to be overly picky at this point in time.

One house had an unopened bag of off-brand dog food, and Avery stowed that away in the trunk of the car. He'd have to check to make sure it hadn't gone moldy, but if it was still fine then Tilly would have food for a few weeks if he made it stretch. That meant the food they were hunting up could last that much longer if it wasn't being rationed between two full grown humans and a beagle. The thought cheered him, and he began to recover from their first dismal stop.

"I wish we had enough gas to drive an RV down south," he mused as they pulled into the driveway of another large home, this one older with a wide front porch and stone steps leading up to it. Parked in the driveway was a monster of a motor home, the type that had a slide out and enough room inside for a family of about six to sleep comfortably. It would have been a dream to get in that thing and drive it off, home always with you no matter where you ended up. He knew that they could never keep the gas tank filled though, the dream dead and gone without even the slightest bit of consideration.

Krissy stared at the thing as they climbed out of the car, letting out a low whistle. "We would be traveling in style, that's for sure. We could fill up the tanks and having running water, and I bet it has a hot water heater too. If it had solar panels that would be the ultimate. We wouldn't even have to be hooked up to electricity to have hot water and air conditioning. That would be the *life*."

Avery let out a quiet groan, and his heart yearned a little bit. What he wouldn't give for that sort of luxury now, after going so long without all those things people took for granted. He wanted to watch a movie while sprawled on the sofa, cook a meal on a proper stove, and take a long hot bath where he turned red as a lobster and scrubbed his skin raw before finally climbing out. They could play video games, have proper lights, and a fridge to keep cold things like fruits and veggies that they gathered up along the way south. The image of a cool, crisp apple made him shiver, but it also brought him out of the fantasy he was losing himself inside of.

"Come on, let's get inside. People have a motor home like that, I bet their house is stocked up with all sorts of good things," he declared, starting for the front door. It was locked tight, which he had anticipated, and the door was solid so he couldn't get in that way. He went around to the back instead, greeted by the sight of a set of sliding glass doors. Turning to Krissy he gestured for her to grab Tilly by the collar, picking up a patio chair as he did so. "Stand back."

Avery swung the chair and then let it fly, watching as it crashed through one of the doors. Glass sprayed everywhere, and the sound was terrific, echoing through the trees behind them a little before dying down. He stepped inside carefully, kicking aside glass shards as Krissy came in behind him carrying Tilly in her arms to keep the dog from getting hurt. The kitchen in this house was vast, the kind that doubled as both a proper kitchen and a second family area. They had a sofa and a loveseat on the other side of the island, a television mounted on the far wall. There were stools at the island, but the table and chairs were located somewhere else entirely which meant there was a dining room. This house was definitely big, and whoever had lived in it had definitely had money.

They started with the top cabinets and worked their way

down, stuffing things they found into the already heavily burdened duffel bag. Canned goods, packages of unopened cookies and crackers, spray cheese, and even a bag of flour. In the walk-in pantry they found two cases of soda, likely gone flat but still worth trying, and a case of bottled water. There was an unopened container of coffee, a package of tea bags, and a still sealed jar of honey.

"We need another bag," Avery decided, not wanting to risk ripping the duffel and having half their food roll away and potentially get ruined. "Let's spread out and see if we can find something."

Krissy began digging around downstairs while Avery headed up, peering into rooms as he went. He found a bathroom and a linen closet before he opened up the door to a bedroom, figuring it had to be the master. There was a huge four-poster bed and an armchair tucked into the corner, someone's clothes still draped over it. He tried two doors and found one to a walk-in closet, spotting a rolling suitcase that would work great. He was pulling it out when he happened to look up, spotting something on a shelf overhead. Reaching up he pulled down a compound bow, like the one he had used growing up. He found the arrows for it in a sheath on the same shelf, and through there were only four of them they were nicely made. He tucked the sheath under his arm and left the room with the bow and the suitcase in two different hands, making a racket as he headed back downstairs.

"Krissy," he yelled out, feeling giddy for the first time in ages. She hurried out of the kitchen and met him in the front hall, eyes wide and frantic. "Look what I found! Isn't it great?"

It took her a moment to register what was going on, looking

at the suitcase and the bow and then back at him. He was clearly pleased with himself, a wide grin on his face, and it was admittedly infectious. She found herself smiling too, reaching out to wrap her fingers around the handle of the suitcase.

"Can you use that thing?" She asked, pulling the case behind her into the kitchen. She unzipped it and started to stuff things inside, glancing up at him as he stood at the counter admiring his find. "You mentioned using one as a kid. Think you could manage to get anything with it?"

"I'm not sure," Avery told her, figuring he might as well be honest about it. Why lie about being able to do something he wasn't sure he could? It made no sense to him, and it was good to just be open right up front. "I want to try though. It could be a game changer! I tried before to set snares and stuff, but it didn't really work out the way I was hoping. I know I'm not good with a gun, but this could be different. I mean you can reuse arrows, and it's definitely quieter. It's weird we were just talking about this and here it was, but maybe it's a sign! Like maybe this was supposed to happen, maybe this is the break I've been waiting for."

"Maybe," Krissy agreed, everything now inside either the suitcase or the duffel bag, both zipped up and ready to go. She pulled them along toward the hallway again, parking them both by the front door. "Did you see anything else useful or are we done here?"

Avery was lost a bit in his own world now, testing the tension in the bow before he noticed she was talking to him again. He cleared his throat a bit and shrugged, a little bit on the sheepish side now. "I didn't really look, I got distracted when I found this. If you want more blankets for your bed or anything there are probably plenty, but I can't think of anything else we really need. I mean we have plenty of first aid supplies and other stuff, food was kind of the main thing we were searching for. We did good here, huh?"

Krissy rolled her eyes but in an amused sort of way, stepping over to take the bow from his hands. "Come on then," she chided him, unlocking the front door. "We can still get another house or two in before we head back to the post office. We have to make the most of it while we're out, right? That's what you said before, and we should stick to that. I'm glad you found something that you think will be useful and that makes you feel good, I know you've been down for a little while, but we still have work to do. You can play with this later."

"You're so bossy," Avery complained, though he followed after her anyway. He carried the duffel and let her roll the suitcase, still holding tight to the sheath of arrows. "A few more houses then, just to see what we can find. I want to get back before it starts to get dark though, I don't like being out after dark. Never have, and never will."

"If that's what you want," Krissy agreed, using the key fob to open the trunk. Together they stored away their spoils and then headed out again, ready to hit up a few more untouched treasures before calling it good. They felt better now for making their little trip, stocked up for a good while longer, and now with the possibility of fresh meat. It was a good start to spring, and it definitely lifted their spirits. They had needed the morale boost, and they had finally blissfully found one.

At the end of the day, as they headed back to Graven, Avery let himself relax. Maybe they really had gotten enough together today to get them through the last stretch, and to have enough left over to start the preparations for the trip. He was eager to start south as soon as the weather turned warm and stayed that way, and though something still felt a little off in the pit of his stomach he was learning to coexist with Krissy. She had proven herself to be rather smart and savvy when she needed to be, and she had good ideas when it got down to brass tacks. He was trusting her a little more every day, which was important and principal to their future survival. He had to let her in, trust her, and to treat her as an equal partner in things. Being alone for so long had made him feel like he could only trust himself, but he was really ready to move on. To do better, to be better, and to make sure they *both* got out of this alive.

SEVENTEEN

THE STOCKPILE WAS LOOKING IMPRESSIVE AGAIN, and Avery was feeling much better about their situation. So much so that they had begun to earnestly plan their trip south, and he had finally settled on a destination. They would head for coastal Georgia first, and if things went well there, they would eventually venture onto Louisiana. Georgia was just momentarily more practical, and it felt good to really have a plan in place. The route was mapped, the supply lists made, and now they just had to wait for May and they would be ready to go. Or, at least, as ready as they were ever going to be considering.

With his confidence returned he decided it was time to try something new, and so he took Tilly and headed into the woods with the bow he had found. Krissy elected to stay behind, probably out of fear of being accidentally shot, willing to work on fixing dinner and preparing storage for any meat he might return with. Neither of them was sure such preparations would even be necessary, but it was better to have it ready to go just in case than to be fumbling around.

The woods around Graven were familiar to Avery, having grown up playing there as a kid. He crossed the bridge and climbed the stairs up the bank near where his house had once sat, deciding it was the best place for his first attempt. This was the area he knew better than any other, familiar ground to both him and Tilly. They made a quick pit stop at the well beside the house, where he drew up the bucket that hadn't been touched in months.

"We forgot to fill the canteen," he chided the beagle, who simply sat on her butt and stared at him. He drew up the bucket and gave the water a good look, noting that it was as clear and cool as it had ever been. The more he thought about it, the less likely it seemed that Jessa could have gotten sick just from drinking from the well. His mother hadn't gotten sick then and neither had his father and it seemed as though he really was immune. Taking the risk he filled the canteen and screwed the lid back on, whistling as he worked. He set off again then, on up the steep incline away from where the house had once sat.

The dog was trotting right alongside him, seeming to know that this outing was different than all those they had previously gone on together. This felt more like old times, the time before Ruger, and her tail was wagging furiously as they stepped into the cool darkness of the woods. Avery breathed in a deep breath of fresh air, his confidence level still high as they weaved their way along the well-worn path. The path had been here, angling between the trees, since long before he had ever been born or before his father had been born even, created by the first people who had settled Graven. They had hunted these woods, picked wild berries, and cut down trees to build their houses. It was a little bit funny in a way, how it had all sort of come full circle. Things had wound their way back to the beginning again, when people had to start relying on nature to get them by and to provide.

Avery thought these quiet, peaceful thoughts to himself as they ambled onward, the hillside leveling out into flat land. It made the going easier and he was able to focus on something else besides not slipping and possibly falling, pausing to listen to the woods. When he had been a kid and his father had been trying to teach him to be a decent hunter, that had always been rule number one. See what the woods had to tell him, see how they felt. There were almost always animals nearby, but you had to listen for the signs and to try and be quiet enough not to spook them off. He had scared off many a critter in his youth, always wanting to be chatty or fidget around. He felt less inclined to do that today though, knowing that this trip was an important one.

"Okay, Till," he whispered to the beagle, who cocked her ears alertly at the sound of her name. "Get in there and stir something up. I hear plenty, mostly little stuff, and you were bred for this. Go find us a rabbit!"

It was almost comical the way she behaved as though she perfectly understood him, taking off at a clip with her nose to the ground. Her big ears flopped around her head as she moved along the path and then off of it, pausing now and then to let out a loud bay. Avery was absolutely thrilled, his hands ready to move with the bow if something came bounding out in front of them. He went off the trail too, trying to stay close to her without stirring up too much racket. When she broke into a run then she got too far ahead of him, disappearing into a stand of thick brush.

"Guess I'll just wait here," he muttered, finding a thick log to sit on. He listened to her barking somewhere in the distance, not too far out but just far enough, and then the sound of something crashing through the woods. Whatever it was it was moving away from him though, to the east, and he cussed under his breath as he stumbled to his feet again. "This way, you damn dog!"

Tilly seemed to be having a grand old time, barking and racing around to her heart's content. Avery was starting to get the feeling that this trip might not prove so fruitful after all, especially when the beagle quit barking altogether. He knew that was probably a sign that she had lost whatever critter she was after and that the trail had gone cold, so he gave her a few minutes to get it together again. When she still didn't bark though he abandoned his log and walked a bit deeper in, listening for signs of her.

"Tilly," he called out, whistling shrilly by using his fingers the way his grandfather had taught him as a kid. "Come on, Till! Let's get going! You aren't in trouble, come on girl! Come on!"

He was met with silence, the kind that made his stomach drop like the hill on a roller-coaster. Something was wrong, and he didn't like the way the air suddenly felt. It was charged, like when a storm was coming, and the hairs on his arms stood up despite him feeling plenty warm. He moved a little deeper into the woods, whistling every few steps to try and draw the beagle to him. She couldn't be lost, she couldn't have gotten that far yet, but what if she was? What if she ran after something so far she couldn't find her way back again? The thought of it was horrifying and he felt like he might burst into tears. That was when he heard her from somewhere to his right, letting a shriek of pain and terror.

"TILLY!"

Avery thought of nothing else but his dog, his constant companion and best friend. He took off at a run, jumping over another fallen log and nearly tripping over the exposed roots of a tree. He cut through brier and bramble, feeling the prickly bits digging into his legs through his pants. A million thoughts crashed through his mind as he ran, his heart pounding furiously inside of his chest. She could have fallen into a hole or gotten stuck in someone's old abandoned trap. What if she was so hurt that he couldn't fix her? He couldn't lose her, it would drive him absolutely mad.

He was still thinking of the myriad possibilities when he stumbled into a clearing, his eyes going to Tilly first and foremost. She was crouched down with her belly to the ground and her tail tucked, a leash looped around her neck and pulled tight as she scrambled to get away. The next thing he noticed was the arm holding the leash, which was attached to a rather tall and broad-shouldered man. He was dressed in black and wearing some sort of body armor that Avery had only ever seen on television before. He had on a black baseball cap and a surgical style mask over his mouth and nose, breathing heavily as he regarded Avery in return.

"It's alright," the man told him, "we don't want to hurt you. We're here to help. Just stay calm and try not to panic, I know this probably feels overwhelming."

The man raised his right fist into the air, and it seemed to be some sort of signal. Several more people dressed in similar black clothes, some of them holding large and imposing weapons, stepped out of the surrounding woods. Avery felt himself starting to sweat, eyes darting between the assembled group of people as he quickly counted their numbers. Six, there were six of them and they were all staring directly at him. There was nowhere to go, nowhere to run, and even if he could have he wouldn't have left Tilly there scared as she was. He didn't blame her, they were a scary lot and it was further compounded by not being able to fully see their faces. Slowly he put the bow down on the ground and held up his hands, trembling a little.

"Let my dog go," he finally managed to get out, Tilly whimpering pitifully now. "She's scared of you and you're hurting her. She's just a little beagle anyway, untie her." He paused and then sucked in a short breath. "Who are you people? Why are you here?"

Seeing Krissy Rawlins outside his door had been a shock but this? This was something else entirely, something he couldn't find words for. How were there so many people here just out of thin air? What were they even doing in a place like Graven? He might have expected to see people like this in a city, but he had certainly never anticipated that such a thing could happen in this little corner of the world.

The man holding Tilly didn't answer, but instead the response came from another man to his left. This one lowered his mask so Avery could see his face, and though it wasn't especially unkind his mouth was set in a thin line and he had a very serious expression. "We're one of the last strongholds of the United States government, a covert branch of the military that has been sent out to find survivors. We've known about you for a while now; one of our scouts spotted you several months back. We wanted to come for you sooner, but the weather was too poor, and we were afraid of getting our equipment stuck. We didn't want to lose sight of you though, so a couple of months ago we did send out a second scout to make sure that you would get through the winter."

"A scout? What are you...talking about..." Avery's words trailed off as realization began to dawn on him. That was when Krissy Rawlins made her appearance, stepping sheepishly out from behind a tree. She gave him a little wave, clearing her throat before she took her own turn to speak.

"I hope you can understand that I didn't *want* to lie to you," Krissy said, looking like she did mean it at least. "It was for your own good though, and you need to understand that as well. The government is trying to find survivors, people who were living out here in the world when the Ruger Virus ravaged everything. These guys, and lots of other government people, were hiding out in airtight bunkers and have taken every precaution to make sure they stay well. You though, Avery, you're so special. You were out here in the thick of it, living in a house with sick and dying people, yet you stayed healthy. If you're truly immune, you could be the key to a cure, or at the very least a vaccine to lessen the future loss of life."

Avery had so many things he wanted to say to her, to scream right in her face, but he swallowed them down. It probably wasn't wise to do such a thing when the people with assault rifles were backing her up. Instead, he took a short step back away from her, his hands still held palms up in the air even though nobody had expressly asked him to do such a thing. "You never wore masks or anything like them, what if you had gotten sick? You could, you know, we went into houses where there were dead bodies and where people had been down with the virus. Weren't you afraid? You potentially exposed yourself."

Krissy just shrugged, though Avery noted that some of the

folks behind her shot glances at each other. He had a feeling that she wasn't supposed to do such a thing, but there was nothing to do about that now. She had taken the chance, and it was her problem going forward. "I volunteered to come, and I knew what the risks involved would be. You could have gotten sick at any time and so could I, but neither of us did. I'll undergo some tests as well when we get back, but for now I just need to know that you're going to trust us. It's important that you do, Avery. I don't want you to have to do this against your will."

"I don't honestly want to do it period," Avery snapped at her, finally dropping his arms back to his sides. "Was it all a lie then? The stupid story about your aunt and the neighbor kids and all of that? Did you just make that up to make me feel sorry for you so I'd let you stay? I knew I should have kicked you out. Even the dog knew what you were! I didn't fully trust you and I forced myself because I thought you were just another hopeless survivor like me!"

A cloud came over Krissy's face then and her jaw set a bit, holding her head a little higher than before. She crossed her arms over her chest, going into full-on defensive mode. "No, it wasn't all a lie. I'm not from nearby, but the rest was the truth. I lost people I loved and cared about, same as you, and I had to watch my friends and neighbors die too. That's when I decided that I had to help, that I had to be part of this to try and figure out a cure. Think of all the people we could save going forward, Avery! That has to be worth something to you!"

"My name is Lieutenant Jonathan Dennings," the man to the right said then, stepping forward so he was standing beside of Krissy. "What Rawlins here is telling you is the truth, kid. We're all sorry that we had to lie to you, that it had to be this way, but we really do need your help. We've only found three survivors so far, including you, and we have to try and figure out what is in your DNA that makes you different. We don't want to see any more people die needless deaths, and deep down I don't think you want that either. You're a smart kid, I saw that myself when Rawlins showed us your hideout. You worked hard, you thought things through, and that means we need you even more. Once we've run some tests, done what we need to, we can give you work. It means a place to stay, food to eat, hot water to bathe in, and a room at the facility where the rest of us live. No more being alone, no more doing this by yourself."

That did give Avery a bit of pause, because it sounded appealing. He knew though that sometimes the best sounding offers were ultimately the worst for you, and that you had to read the fine print so to speak. Volunteering to just go with these strangers was a convoluted idea, something he couldn't fathom as nice as it did sound. He wanted to go back to his post office, back to his plans for traveling south for the winter. He wanted a little house with a garden, with plenty of fishing and hunting and room for Tilly to run. What if he got there and it was all a lie? What if they just wanted to chop him up like some experiment?

"Let my dog go," Avery said finally, looking at poor Tilly again. She was choking herself straining against the leash looped around her neck, and he wanted to just reach out and grab her. "Can't you see she's in distress? You people are strangers, she doesn't trust you."

Lieutenant Dennings turned to the man holding the leash and nodded his head once. The man stepped forward and leaned down, untying the leash from the beagle's neck. Tilly fled to Avery who scooped her up in his arms, holding her trembling body tightly as he looked at each of them in turn. His eyes lit on Krissy last, shaking his head at her in disgust.

"You should have just told the truth. You should have told me where you were from, and that there were others. How am I supposed to trust you or your heavily armed buddies while knowing how badly you lied to me? You made me think you were like me, that you had come from a similar situation as me, but you didn't. Not really. You lost people, sure, but everyone has done that. You didn't struggle like I did, you had the freaking government feeding and taking care of you. There's no way I'm going anywhere with you," he told her bitingly, taking another step back.

This time Lieutenant Dennings stepped forward, not giving Avery the chance to retreat further, holding his gun a little more tightly. "Come on, Mr. Harris. We don't want it to be like this, nobody does. It would be better for all of us if you just came along without putting up a fight. Using force is the last thing we want to do, but we will do it if you push us to. We were ordered to bring you back and we're going to follow orders."

Avery nodded in understanding as he steeled himself and then he ran, Tilly still in his arms. He just bolted, dodging back between the trees in the direction he had come from. He heard them giving chase, crashing through the underbrush as they tried to catch up to him. He could hear Dennings voice yelling out for nobody to shoot, to take him alive and as uninjured as possible, which gave him that much more hope. If they couldn't shoot then he had a pretty fair shake of it, especially if he could make it into one of the houses well ahead of them. Most had an attic space, perfect for hiding. He and Tilly could both squeeze in, where the only real trouble would be keeping the beagle quiet until they were gone.

He was immensely hopeful as he sprinted, seeing the break in the tree line where the woods met the sloping hillside just ahead of him. He was so close, nearly there, when he slipped on a wet patch of leaves. He pitched backward as he fell, Tilly tumbling out of his arms and rolling away from him. He lay on his back trying to catch his breath, the wind knocked out of him. The next thing he heard was Krissy's voice trying to soothe Tilly, slipping another lead around her neck as she leaned over him.

"You shouldn't have run," she reprimanded him, one of her masked companions appearing in his line of sight now too. "You really shouldn't have, Avery, it would have just been better for you to comply. We aren't going to hurt you or the dog, okay? I've never tried to hurt either of you, and I don't intend to start now."

The masked person had pulled a needle and syringe out of a pack they were carrying now, uncapping it as he watched. He started writhing and trying to scoot backward, away from the two of them, but his feet could find no real purchase in the wet soil. "Stop it," he groaned, Tilly crawling over to him and licking his face. "Leave us alone. Just leave us alone!"

"I'm afraid we can't do that," the masked person, a woman, spoke to him. "I'm a nurse, and I wish I could tell you that this won't hurt a bit but that could be a lie. It might hurt, but I assure you it's completely unintentional."

Krissy rolled up the sleeve of his shirt and then he felt the needle pressing into his skin. That part didn't hurt, but the actual injection did. Whatever she had put into his body burned as it entered, and almost immediately he felt light-headed and woozy.

Everything that came after the shot was a blur, just bits and pieces managing to penetrate the haze and register with his tired brain.

He felt himself being lifted and put on a stiff board before rising into the air. It was a bumpy trip, three of the men carrying him through the woods and out to a huge open field. There were several large armored vehicles there, including one that was used for medical evacuations. He was loaded into that one along with poor Tilly who climbed onto the board with him and laid against his chest. His arms were tied down so he couldn't hug or pet her, but having her there was a comfort and he was glad for it.

"Shouldn't be too much longer to the helicopter."

The vehicle was moving, but for how long he didn't know. He'd been in and out too much, the concept of time long gone. The person who spoke was near his head though, answered by someone else who seemed impossibly far away.

"Yeah, we'll go back with him and the others will keep on looking. If we're lucky we'll find more like him, it gives us more opportunities for a cure or a vaccine."

"-think it's possible?"

"Maybe."

The conversation began to break up into pieces, and he couldn't connect anymore dots. He fell back asleep, though he began to come around when he felt himself being jostled again. He heard the rotors of the helicopter and felt the wind from it ruffling his hair and clothes as they loaded him in through an open cargo hatch in the back. This wasn't a small tourist helicopter but was instead some big military ordeal which didn't honestly surprise him. They were military, after all, people working for the government. It made sense that they would have a big Apache deal to move around in, even if it was sort of a waste of fuel.

Tugging at the restraints he tried his level best to sit up, his mouth dry and his anger returning. He felt sore all over from his fall, and his head ached something fierce. He didn't care about that though, what he cared about was suddenly getting himself free, rocking the backboard back and forth so hard it smacked against the floor. That had been the wrong move as one of the soldiers appeared, not in a mask now, scowling at him openly.

"Rogers," the guy called out gruffly, gesturing to someone outside the cargo door. "He's waking up! Give him another dose!"

"No," Avery eked out, voice scratchy from his dry throat. "NO!"

The last thing he heard was Tilly barking and the woman who had administered the first shot, obviously named Rogers, loudly complaining as she shoved another needle in his arm. This time he went out hard and stayed that way, borne away from the world on a wave of anesthetic.

EIGHTEEN

AVERY HAD NO IDEA HOW MUCH TIME HAD LAPSED when he finally came to, blurry eyes flickering open and then immediately closing again against a garish artificial light above him. Dots were swimming behind his eyelids and he rubbed at them furiously, taking in a few quick breaths before he opened them again, this time using his hand as a shield. His head hurt and felt swimmy as he sat up, and for a second he thought he might be sick. He got the urge under control though and finally opened his eyes the rest of the way, getting a good look at the room he was in.

It was completely unfamiliar in every way, no place he had ever been even before the Ruger Virus had hit. The walls were all stark white without a single piece of art or even a window, the floors black and white checked tile that were too shiny and reflected back the overhead lighting. The bed he was on sat in the middle of the room, covered in overly starched sheets and blankets. At his feet lay Tilly, lifting her head as he stirred and staring at him with her brow furrowed with worry. He reached down to pet her, eyes still sweeping the room.

Up near the ceiling in the corner by the door he saw the camera, which moved slowly from side to side as it took in the entire room. Beside it was a small speaker, obviously so people outside the room could communicate with him. If anyone had noticed that he was awake yet they hadn't bothered to say anything, and he was okay with that. Talking would likely just make his already aching head hurt even worse.

The place had a smell to it too, something he had at least come in contact with before. It had the same overly bleached and sterile smell of the hospital he had visited as a kid when his grandmother had been battling cancer, the sort of smell you never really forgot. It made sense that they would want the place to be as sanitized as possible if they were truly dealing with the Ruger Virus, but the bleachy smell added to his queasiness.

In the end he laid back down, pressing the heels of his hands against his eyes and swallowing thickly. What was he doing here? Where was here anyway? He didn't feel any different than before besides the headache brought on by the drugs they had used to knock him out, so he was fairly certain they probably hadn't done any tests on him yet. Though if he had been unconscious they could have done plenty of things and he'd have no recollection of them at all. The mere idea of it made him feel violated and dirty, shivering a little as he dropped his hands to stare up at the ceiling.

"I'd like some answers please," he called out finally, speaking into the room in hopes that someone, somewhere, might hear him. "Would someone like to tell me what's going on?"

His voice faded and the room felt quiet again, the only sound one of a fan running somewhere nearby pumping fresh air into the room. Finally the speaker in the corner crackled to life and he sat up again, mouth set into a thin line as a recorded voice began speaking to him.

"Welcome to emergency management research facility number four, Alexandria, Virginia. We here at EMRF are dedicated to studying and eradicating diseases responsible for global pandemics and widespread loss of life. Currently we are studying the impact of the Ruger Virus on global populations and are interested in both a cure and preventative vaccination possibilities. This is a decontamination facility, outfitted with the latest technology to help prevent the spread of infectious disease, and is the safest place to be in the event of worldwide catastrophe. Your health and happiness are of the utmost concern, and we urge you to remain patient until a staff member can address your individual needs. Have a great day!"

That was it, the entire thing, and Avery felt angrier than ever. They had attacked him, forced him here against his will, and they couldn't even answer him directly? All they had given him was a crummy recording that had left him with more questions than answers. It was enough to get him out of bed though, feet hitting the cold floor since he had on no socks. He didn't even have his own clothes on, dressed instead in a pair of paper-thin white pants and a matching shirt with small buttons on the front. It was as though they had slipped him into the world's worst pair of pajamas before tossing him into this cell-like room.

He began to pace then, making loops around the room from corner to corner. It gave him something to focus on at least, a place to channel his current rage and anger. He might have kept at it for hours, he had absolutely no concept of time at all, but he was finally interrupted by a buzz at the door. Someone called out for him to get back and so he did, retreating to the far wall as the door swung open and a woman wearing scrubs and a lab coat appeared. She was carrying a tray in her hands, stepping into the room and sitting it on the bed. She paused then to get a look at Avery, glancing him up and down in an appraising sort of way.

"You're finally awake, that's good. I was starting to think they had overdosed you when they knocked you out. I told them to be careful with you, they're supposed to be careful with all the test subjects, but they think that brute force is as careful as they can be," she said, rolling her eyes a little. "I'm Doctor Selena Dobrev, I'm a member of the EMRF and one of the lead scientists working on a cure for the Ruger Virus. I'm sure you were already informed that we're seeking out immune individuals to help us with our goal?"

Avery smelled the scent of food wafting from the tray and his stomach growled considerably. He nodded his head slowly though, not daring to take a single step forward. "Yes, well, sort of. They told me that they needed people like me to try and figure out what makes us immune. I do have a question of my own though. How did none of you get sick? Are you immune or what?"

Doctor Dobrev actually laughed at that, shaking her head a little. "No, no, we're not immune. Not that we know of, anyway, but we've also never been exposed to the virus outside of a controlled laboratory setting. We knew about the release of the virus, and we knew of its intended purpose, but once it got out of control and began to spread on its own in a mutated form we immediately came to one of the bunkers. These types of places exist all over the country, all over the world really, to house top government officials and people like myself so that we're protected and out of danger. I know it sounds awful considering so many have died, but it's necessary. We have to keep our government as functional as possible and in the case of a pandemic like this one, we need scientists like me to get things back on track. Which is where you come in."

"Wait. Release of the virus? What does that mean?" Avery asked her then, starting to see the bigger picture more and more clearly. He was sincerely hoping he was wrong in his assumptions, but he just had a feeling that his thought process was more on track than ever.

"It wasn't supposed to be like this," she tried to assure him, moving her position to be a little more near the still open door. "We were seeking an answer to population control, in a way that we never had to before. People are living longer, staying healthier, and it's causing a lot of unanticipated problems across the world. The Ruger Virus was intended to be one of the first steps in solving global warming, among other issues, but it went terribly wrong. The virus was deadly, yes, but only to very specific facets of the population. Primarily it was meant to target the elderly, the immunocompromised, and those whose lives are no longer considered viable. It worked well at the offset; nobody even really noticed anything unusual was going on. Then at some point the virus began to mutate, and that pig farmer in Louisiana picked it up. After that it spread like wildfire, and we were forced back to the drawing board to create something to stop the avalanche we had already started."

Avery reached out to balance himself with a hand on the wall, feeling as though his legs might go out from under him. He was staring at Doctor Dobrev with a look of horror on his face, trying to come to terms with everything he had just been told. Over and over again the news had reported that nobody knew the origins of the virus that not even the CDC had an answer, and it had all been a lie. A lie orchestrated and put into motion by their own government as a way of controlling them without their knowledge. It was absolutely depraved, worse than anything he could have imagined, head shaking almost of its own accord now.

"How could you do that?" He asked her then, still leaning into the wall. "How could you set something like that out? It doesn't even matter that it changed into something you didn't intend, you did it to begin with and that's sick! It wasn't up to any of you to play God, but you did and look what happened! You did this horrible thing, and then everyone else in the world paid the price. Now you just expect that we'll help you that you can use the few of us that are left to fix your shitty mistakes!"

"I understand your anger, I really do. If I could take it back I would, but I can't. All we can do now is try to move forward and, yes, you are a key component in that process. We need you, Avery, so that we can make sure nobody else has to die because of our mistake," Dobrev told him then, clearly trying to win him back over to her side of things. "I'm aware that you lost your family, and for that I'm deeply sorry. I know that won't ever make it right, won't ever make your life the way it was, but I still am. Please, help us. We've only found a handful of people like you so far, and we need to study all of you in order to solve this. It's like a puzzle, and you're one of the pieces we need to put it all together."

Avery knew she was making it sound good; trying to appeal

to the side of him that didn't want others to have to suffer. He also knew though that she, and all the others, were liars and that they could never be totally trusted. "What kind of tests?" He asked finally, figuring he might as well know before he either committed or refused.

Doctor Dobrev looked relieved at that, giving him a faint smile of hope. "Well, we've already started with a few blood tests. We took some samples while you were out, to make it less painful for all of us involved. We're trying to figure out what you and the others have that makes you different, what is keeping you from catching the virus. Once we have a better idea, then we'll do some other tests. Mostly health related things, to see if you have similar body types and physiology in common. At some point we may need to inject some subjects with the virus itself, to see if it's a true immunity or if you'll exhibit some of the symptoms and become a carrier. Those tests will be completed by tomorrow, and we'll have a few early answers by then."

"What will happen when the testing ends?" Avery implored then, finally pushing himself away from the wall. The food was enticing him, and he made his way to the bed where he sat. He uncovered the plates and found sausages, mashed potatoes, macaroni and cheese, and a large piece of warm apple pie. He gave a sausage to Tilly and bit into one himself, waving his fork at Doctor Dobrev so she would continue and answer his question.

"That all depends on what we find. As a subject you'll remain here in the facility with us until we've fully developed a vaccination or a potential cure, or even both if we're lucky. All those who are held in the facility and aren't immune, like myself, will take the vaccine and be able to integrate back into the world. As will you, once we're at that stage. If we manage to work out a cure, then anyone who falls ill going forward will be administered a dose at onset and will eventually get well again," she explained, trying to put it as simply as she could. "It's going to take a long time for the world to rebuild itself; we're starting from scratch almost. It will take an enormous amount of work from all of us."

"I'm not sure I like this," Avery finally decided, working on the mashed potatoes now after giving Tilly two more sausages, since she was just as hungry as he was. "I mean what you're saying sounds good, obviously, but you people also have a pretty sordid history here. You started this, and now you're trying to save face. Not that it matters, since most of the world is pretty much dead at this point. I can't trust that this is it, that you just want to do some blood tests and stuff on me and then feed me until it's time to move back out into the world. I get the feeling it doesn't really work that way, and I'd personally rather just go back to Graven and my life. It wasn't much, but it was mine and I worked hard for it. That's the option I think I'd like to choose."

Doctor Dobrev let out a very weary sounding sigh, pinching the bridge of her nose between her thumb and index finger. She shook her head a little and reached for the doorknob with her free hand, clearly displeased with him. "I'm really sorry again, Avery, but that isn't going to happen. I was hoping that after having a real, honest talk with you that you would see the right side of things and just make this easy. Krissy warned me that it probably wouldn't happen like that, but I wanted to at least make an attempt to prove her wrong. I guess I was the fool on that one. We are moving forward one way or another, and if that means putting you under every time we have to take something from you then we will. It makes me sad it has to be that way."

Avery dropped his fork and slid from the bed again, pointing his finger at her sharply. "You see? You just made my point! This isn't about me or what I want, or even what's best for everyone else! This is about you people getting what you want out of us, and nothing more! I don't care if you ever find a cure, I don't care if all of you have to spend the rest of your miserable lives in this bunker until the day you all die! It's what you deserve!"

"We'll speak again soon." That was all Doctor Dobrev said to him as she stepped out, shutting and locking the door behind her. He charged it and began to beat his fists against it, leaving Tilly to eat the rest of the food on the tray. His appetite was gone now anyway, his stomach too sour to take it.

"Let me out of here," he screamed, throwing his entire weight into the door now. It moved a little but didn't give, fastened tight and solid from the outside. "Let me out! You can't keep me here, I'm not a prisoner! I'm a human being, I still have rights! Let me out now!"

He wasn't really sure if he had rights left or not, or how that sort of thing worked in times like these. Had basic human rights and privileges gone out the window with the downfall of the modern world? It was very possible and probable, whether he liked it or not. They could do what they wanted with him here, where there was nobody who knew him or to advocate for him. They were the important people anyway, the ones who had always called the shots and who still called them even now. He didn't have to like it or appreciate it, he just had to deal with it and accept it.

Avery screamed until his throat went hoarse, finally going back to his abandoned bed. He threw the tray onto the floor, scattering bowls and silverware across the pristine tile. He was crying by the time he laid down, Tilly crawling up the mattress on her belly to lick his face. He wrapped his arms around her and cried into her fur, realizing that they would never leave this place. They were trapped here for as long as these people wanted them to be, locked inside of this sterile room and poked and prodded on. A day might come, far from now, when they were finally let go but that might never come to fruition either. It was entirely likely that nobody would ever figure out a cure or a vaccine, and this would be it. This would just be it for forever until the very end.

NINETEEN

AFTER EXHAUSTING HIMSELF BY SCREAMING AND crying, Avery fell into a fitful sleep. His headache slipped away though, and when he woke again the fluorescent lights overhead had been dimmed a little. It made the room feel less like a hospital ward though, which he could appreciate, and another tray of food had been left on the floor inside the door. He fetched it and shared the cheeseburger and fries with Tilly, enjoying having real meat again. It had been so long since they'd had food that wasn't from a can, and despite the way he felt inside at all of them, this part wasn't so bad.

They had even left him a few books in a neat stack, all classics and all worn out, but books were books and it was at least entertainment. He wasn't sure how they had known to leave them but he wasn't complaining, reclining back on the stiff mattress and cracking open Heart of Darkness. He felt achy and he wished for his air bed, calling out to the people behind the speaker to ask if they could turn the fan up a little. The room had gotten stuffier as the hours had droned by, and they at least complied and pumped in a little more cool air.

He was still there reading, Tilly resting with her head on his stomach, when his door buzzed open for the second time during his waking hours. He peered over the top of the book and was not surprised to see Krissy Rawlins there, dressed in blue scrubs like the doctor had worn with her hair pulled back into a messy ponytail. She looked tired but resolved, the door shutting behind her as she made her way across the room. Without invitation or permission she sat down on the mattress by his feet, sitting in silence for a long moment before she spoke.

"I've already apologized for lying to you, but let me say one more time that I'm sorry. I was hoping that you'd understand once you heard everything, and that you would want to help. I thought that you'd see why I had to lie at first, why I couldn't just come out with the truth, and it bothers me that you can't seem to come around to that. Just know though that if I hadn't thought lying was necessary I never would have done it, and that I thought our friendship was at least real," she told him, tapping the cover of the book with her finger. "I told them you read a lot to pass the time, so they let me send you these. Whenever they move you to another room though you'll have a television, so you can at least watch movies."

Avery wasn't sure he cared much about being able to watch television, and he didn't look as excited about the perk of having one as Krissy seemed to want him to be. Instead he just shrugged, turning down a corner of the page to mark his place before closing the book and laying it aside. "A friendship built on lies can't be real, what part of that don't you understand? You deceived me, on purpose, and then you let them bring me here. I never wanted this, Krissy, and you were with me there for months so I know you at least came to understand that part of me. I had plans, I had things I wanted to do, and this was not on the list. They won't let me leave here, they're holding me hostage. You helped them do that, so therefore I hate you by proxy."

Krissy sucked in a deep breath at the word hate, eyes narrowing a bit into a glare. She wanted to yell at him but she didn't, giving herself a moment to calm down before she gave her rebuttal. "Someday, you will see that this is the best thing, Avery. What they're doing here is for the betterment of the world, it's bigger than all of us. The government is trying to put the pieces back together, to get it all back to the way it should be. You get to be part of that, and I really thought that would trump everything else. You acted like this genuinely good person who took in a stranger, who couldn't stand to see another person suffering. Yet here you are, willing to let other people suffer and die so you can...do what? Run off to Georgia? Life on a beach somewhere until you get old and die? I don't see how you can't want to make a difference!"

"Because none of this means anything," Avery finally snapped, leaning up to jab her sharply in the shoulder. "It could take them years to figure this out, and by then there won't even be anyone left out there to save! If there even is anyway! The only reason they want to figure this out is to save their own asses, to vaccinate and cure themselves so they can stay alive long enough to pat themselves on the back. It's their fault this happened in the first place, they loaded the gun and then they pulled the trigger! They can't just backtrack and put a Band-Aid over what they did. It doesn't work like that! The old world is done. It's gone, there is no getting it back. I don't want to be part of their new world order, giving them a second chance to mess it up all over again. They've done enough, Krissy, truly."

"You're just selfish," Krissy hissed, getting back to her feet. "Maybe I should have had them just leave you out there to rot, eating your canned food in your shitty post office, waiting on spring to come so you could find reasons to put off your trip. You were never leaving there, Avery, so don't pretend you ever were. Talking about it was all well and good, but you are the type who is too afraid to pull the trigger. At least they were willing to take a risk for the rest of us, even if it backfired. They're going to take what they need from you anyway, so I guess it doesn't even matter about what kind of person you are. In the end, it all balances itself out."

She started for the door, muttering to herself as she went. She had just reached for the knob when Avery spoke again, voice much more evenly toned and with far less passion than before.

"We're all going to end up the same," he told her, watching her shoulders tense up as he spoke. "None of us are making it off this rock alive, and you know that. You've always known that, and it scares you so you're clinging to false hope. You know I'm right when I say none of this means anything, and you hate it. Just let that sink in for a little while."

Avery picked his book up again as she left the room, slamming the door shut behind her. Once she was gone, no longer able to hear footsteps or movement outside the door, he began to laugh. He put the book down again and rested his hand on Tilly's head instead, stroking her velvety soft ears. The cooler air in the room wasn't cooling him down in the least, and he knew that the fever was coming on strong. When he coughed he coughed into a tightly closed voice, keeping as quiet as possible to try and hide the situation from the people in the control room who were watching and listening to his every move.

The fever had started sometime in his sleep, and he had figured out quickly that the aching his bones was not from the stiff mattress. By now Krissy Rawlins was traipsing her way through the facility, carrying his germs to all their nice, sterilized places and to each person that she met. She hadn't been sure whether or not she was immune, but he was going to guess that she wasn't. Just like he wasn't either, and apparently had never been. He had just been lucky, done the right things to keep himself well despite being around the sick and dying.

The well water was all he could think of, having filled his canteen up with it before heading into the woods with Tilly on the day he had been taken. He had taken several long drinks so of that good, cold, untreated water and had invited the pathogens into his body. Or maybe it had been something else, maybe the wrong trip into the wrong house where there were dead people locked up with their germs swimming around in the air. He didn't know for sure, there was no way of knowing at all now, but it was hilarious. Absolutely and utterly hilarious, given the circumstances.

In a place like this, sealed up tight with everyone in close quarters, it wouldn't take Ruger long to spread. Quite a lot where likely to be infected before they ever even figured it out. Of course by that point he'd be dead already and wouldn't have to care, laughing again as the beagle stared at him with her big, brown eyes.

"Don't worry, Till," he whispered to her, kissing the end of her wet nose gently. "It's almost over. Almost over now, not much longer and then we're free."

More laughter was accompanied by another fit of coughing, a little blood coming up this time. They had wanted a test subject and, oh, had they gotten one.

RAG & BONE

ASHES

ONE

August 2017

IT WAS AN UNBEARABLY HOT DAY IN PASADENA, just like the day before that, and the day before that. They were in the middle of a heat wave, and the fourth day of August was turning out to be no different. It was the kind of heat that made you see ripples in the air above the pavement, and that left the grass parched and scratchy feeling. Not that the Jacobs family had much of a lawn to speak of these days, as the oppressive heat and current drought meant that the yard wasn't getting the attention it really deserved. Sarah Jacobs knew that it drove her mother, Yolanda, absolutely insane to have her flowerbeds withering away, but the city said that there was no water to waste and they had to each do their part.

Despite the heat, Sarah and her twin brother, Trey, were already outside just after nine that morning ready to take on the neighborhood. They had a small group of friends who lived on their street, and they had all taken to meeting up early at the nearby baseball diamond. None of them were on a little league team, and didn't particularly want to be. They saw baseball as a way to pass the time before the sun got too high overhead, and not as something they had to do out of obligation. It was just for fun more than competition, or at least that was what the winning team always said when the other team got sore at them for it.

They left home on their bicycles with a promise that they would be home for lunch, cutting across a few of their neighbors' backyards to get them to the field that much sooner. Their friends had already assembled by the time they arrived, tossing around the ball and bragging like they were all future professionals of the sport. Sarah and Trey fell easily into the conversation, joking and laughing like they'd been there the entire time. It all just came easily, it was natural, and Sarah didn't know it then but she would never forgot that day.

It would stay forever ingrained in her memory. The last truly good, carefree day she would have for a long time. Maybe, it would seem later on, for forever.

The kids played ball until a quarter to twelve, sweat dripping in their eyes, and dust sticking to their limbs. They were dirty and tired but also satisfied, breaking up to head to their respective homes for the midday meal. They promised each other to meet back up again at dusk at Darryl's house, where his parents would allow them all to use the fire pit to make s'mores, before scattering on their bikes again.

Sarah and Trey raced each other back to their modest ranch style home, with its currently brown front lawn and single shady white alder tree. They propped their bikes up against said tree and them clamored into the house, shoving each other and babbling happily about the get together that evening and whether or not mama would let them actually go.

They found Yolanda in the kitchen sitting on a stool by the counter, watching the news on the small television she kept there. She liked to watch talk shows while she cooked, she claimed it kept her good company, though what she was watching now wasn't her normal recorded episode of the View or the noon update of the local news. This was the world news, and Sarah knew that because she recognized the anchor. It was an older white woman with limp brown hair, who spoke with a droning and monotonous tone. She was so boring she almost put Sarah to sleep, which was just another reason to avoid the evening world news at all costs.

"Mama, what did you make us for lunch? I'm starving," Trey blurted out, interrupting their mother's rather intense concentration. He had his head stuck in the fridge as he peered around inside for something to eat, tapping his foot impatiently against the tile floor just like their father, Marcel, did.

Yolanda turned on her stool then, looking almost startled as though she hadn't heard come in until Trey had spoken to her. She turned the volume down a little on the television, then gestured for two plates sitting at the other end of the counter. "Some sandwiches. Chips are in the cabinet, and you can pour your own juice," she told them, turning her attention right back to the news again.

That was what really weirded Sarah out, seeing how indifferent her mother seemed at the moment. Normally she would fuss over them, forcing them to scrub their hands and arms clean before they so much as looked at her dinner table or even thought about eating. She usually would balk at their dirty clothes and implore them to change after they ate, immediately stuffing the dirty items into the washing machine to avoid any stains setting in. Today she did none of that though, shoved them over a handful of napkins without so much as looking up again.

"Weird," Sarah muttered to Trey as she grabbed the napkins and then got two glasses from the cabinet, filling them with apple juice. She took those to the table while her brother got the plates and a bag of chips, both of them tucking into the food like they were absolutely ravenous and hadn't eaten in days. Playing out in the hot sun just took it out of a kid, and they needed to refuel if they were going to make it through their afternoon chores, which included cleaning their bedrooms and the bathroom that they shared.

They were quietly bickering over who would have to clean the toilet when their mother's cell phone rang, going silent so they could hear who she was speaking to. Sarah could tell by her tone that it was her father, Marcel, her mother speaking low as they weren't sitting just across the room and could hear perfectly fine.

"Did you see the news? Isn't that wild?" Yolanda asked, lips pressed together a bit more. She turned the sound up a bit, leaning her elbows on the counter with the phone still to her ear. "Some kind of super flu or something, they're saying. Some pig farmer in Louisiana got it, they think from pig shit. Just be careful, okay? Just tell them no if they want you to haul any livestock. I mean it, Marcel!"

Sarah turned to her brother then, still keeping her voice low. "Some guy got sick from a pig?" She asked him, unsure if he'd heard anything about such a thing. Trey was a big-time gamer, and spent most of his summer evenings with a headset on in front of his Xbox. He talked to all sorts of other gamers, and got all kinds of good gossip from just about everywhere. She was a bit let down then when Trey shook his head, finishing off the last bite of his sandwich.

"I don't know what she's talking about," he shrugged, reaching for the bag of chips and pouring more onto his plate. "Who cares though? I mean so what if some guy got sick from having sex with a pig or something? I mean it's his business, isn't it?"

"First of all, that's gross. Second of all, I don't think that's how get you a disease from animals," Sarah snorted, rolling her eyes at her brother. She and Trey had just recently turned fifteen, and it seemed to her that suddenly everything he talked about somehow came back around to sex. It was weird, and she didn't like it all. "Also it's obviously upsetting mom, and you know it's because of daddy's job."

Marcel Jacobs had a job driving cargo up and down the California coast, moving products from point A to point B. Before they were born he'd been a long-haul trucker, traveling all over the country, but since he'd settled down with a family he only took short jobs that didn't have him leaving the state. Every now and then he'd be gone overnight, but most evenings he was back home with them by supper time. He always had stories for them about the stuff he hauled, everything from tomatoes and fresh fruit to cars and big machinery. He had hauled animals a few times too, though Sarah didn't like to think about that. It made her sad to imagine pigs and cows crammed into long trailers, and it was even worse when she let herself remember where they were going.

Trey just waved off her concerns as he got to his feet, finishing up his last handful of chips. "Relax, Sarah. Mama worries about everything, it's not a big deal. Dad will be fine anyway, he hasn't hauled live cargo in months. Even if he did though, he's perfectly safe. I mean he just drives the truck, it's not like he's back there in the trailer with the animals or something. I'm going to go get started on my room, I don't want to waste all evening on it."

Sarah just sighed and finished her own lunch, gathering up her own dishes and those that her twin had left behind. She deposited everything in the sink and put the chip bag back in the pantry, pausing as she started past her mother. She leaned over to kiss her mom on the cheek, which elicited a warm smile from Yolanda. The phone call was over, but Sarah could still see the worry in her mom's eyes as she left her there and headed upstairs.

She made a mental note to herself to look up about the pig farmer and his illness later, wanting to know a little more about it. As the day wore on, however, the information was slowly lost. Sarah focused on cleaning her room and her share of the bathroom, and then taking a shower before heading over to Darryl's house for s'mores and hanging out. In those long hours she forgot completely about the farmer, about the pigs, and about the worry on her mother's face. Her dad was home in time for dinner, and they all bantered together and talked about their days. Any inclination she'd had that something might be wrong up and disappeared, lost to the routine business of a summer's day.

TWO

August 2017

IT WAS NEARLY TWO WEEKS BEFORE THE FIRST case of what was now being called the Ruger Virus, named after the scientist who had first discovered exactly what it was, showed up in the state of California. A woman named Lucille Billings has brought it back with her from a vacation in Texas, and it was all over the news. It wasn't an immediate cause for concern, however, until it began to locally spread. One case became two, then six, then ten. Before long it had spread to Los Angeles, a group of YouTube stars who lived in a house together all contracting it and passing it quickly to their friends. From there it was like lighting an unstoppable wildfire that nobody could get under control.

  To Sarah it seemed as though her mother was constantly glued to the television watching the news, and if she wasn't in front of one of their sets she was catching updates on her phone. With every day that passed without a confirmed case in Pasadena Yolanda seemed to be able to get her breath, though she never fully relaxed. Sarah knew that her father had noticed it too, always encouraging her mother to put the phone down and step away from the news for little bits of time. They went on their usual evening walks, and sometimes sat out on the porch in the evenings with a beer or glass of wine. It wasn't much, but the breaks were necessary for the sanity of the entire family.

"Mom is obsessed," Trey had declared on a particularly bad day, when Los Angeles saw its first Ruger related deaths. It was three of the YouTubers, all of them relatively young and supposedly very healthy. They had succumbed fast too, or so it seemed, and that had renewed their mother's seemingly constant need to be informed. "What good does it do to know though? I heard there isn't a cure or anything."

"Because if we know then maybe we can stay safe," Sarah retorted, regurgitating the argument her mother had given her father just the night before. He had expressed a sentiment similar to Trey's, and her mother hadn't been happy with that at all. Yolanda believed that knowledge was power, and though Marcel had a very different outlook on the situation he had at least known when to let it go.

There was no arguing with Yolanda Jacobs; she was the type of woman who loved to have the final word. Sarah and Trey's grandmother, Nana Bee, insisted that she had always been that way. As a child she had lived to argue with her brother, and would carry on until she was read in the face if she didn't get her way. In those days Yolanda's brother, their uncle Ramon, would just egg her on by saying something else every time the fight was winding down just to get her going again. That certainly didn't happen these days, as Marcel wasn't one for bickering and would always just agree to disagree to end the fight sooner rather than later.

Sarah could see her mother's point though, really and truly. If they knew where the cases were, and if sick people were spreading it, then they'd known if it was nearby. Then they could take some sort of action, though she was at a loss as to what that action might be. It wasn't as though something like this had happened before in her lifetime, or her parents either, and that any of them knew exactly what was to be done. Even Nana Bee wasn't sure, though she encouraged Yolanda to keep herself informed while also not scaring the children.

Their mother didn't have to scare them though, because their friends were on top of that. All anybody wanted to talk about now was Ruger, and what was happening all across the country. There were some places that were absolutely teeming with it now, and nobody was any closer to figure out how to slow the spread of it. Louisiana, where the virus had begun, was hit particularly hard and a lot of people had already died there. It was a frightening concept, and one that nobody could get enough of. At the baseball diamond, the ice cream truck, and when hanging out in each other's backyards the others were seemingly preoccupied with talking about it.

"Did you guys see that a couple of kids died in Mississippi?" Darryl asked, everyone spread out on the grass beneath a huge shade tree in his backyard. They were all sucking on Otter Pops, watching the leaves rustle overhead. It was another hot day, too hot for much of anything else, and nobody immediately answered him. They were flagging in the heat, even with the cool treat.

Finally Caroline, who lived two streets over, answered him after slurping up the remaining dredges of her popsicle. "I heard it liquefies your insides," she told them, seemingly very serious in her statement. "My older brother, Keith, he told me so. He's watched a bunch of videos about it online and stuff. He said it's true, and he doesn't tell many lies."

Trey rolled over on his stomach then, resting his chin on his crossed arms. His own otter pop was gone, the plastic discarded on the grass. "I thought Ebola did that," he said, making a face at the thought. "Maybe it's the same thing. They don't know much about it, right? I mean it could be the same sort of disease or something. Like it liquefies your guts and you bleed all over the place and then you die. That would be so gnarly."

"You guys shouldn't believe crap you see online, and neither should Keith," Sarah chimed in, sitting up with her half-eaten pop still in her hand. "That's how rumors and lies spread, and then people get upset. I don't think it turns your insides to goo, I think you just get really sick and then you don't get better again. Or most people don't. I mean it can't kill everybody, right?"

Sarah knew that something like that, that killed everyone, was called an extinction event. Or at any rate that was what the guy on the news program her mother watched regularly now called it. It seemed totally impossible and implausible, a disease that killed everyone. How could that just happen? It didn't make any sense at all, not even a little bit. Though she also knew that a couple of cases had cropped up in other countries where people from the United States had traveled without knowing they were sick. Most everywhere had closed their borders to them now, and there was nowhere to go. They didn't even want folks traveling from state to state now if they could help it, though people did. People were leaving the cities for other places with less people, she'd heard her mom and dad talking about it. Her mother wasn't opposed to the idea, but her father was.

That was an argument that hadn't been resolved, and that her father hadn't caved on. The first time in recent memory for Sarah that her mother hadn't gotten what she'd wanted.

Though it had to be noted that her mother had still bought supplies to store in the garage, just in case. Yolanda called it her stockpile, and Marcel hadn't said a word about it. There was canned food, a camp stove with a box of small propane gas canisters to keep it running, bottles upon bottles of drinking water, flashlights, batteries, and more. She had several totes with blankets, pillows, spare clothes, and other goods tucked inside as though preparing to leave at a moment's notice. It felt very doomsday prepper of her, but Sarah found that it gave her a bit of comfort. If something did happen then they could leave. They could just take off without looking back, and quickly if need be. Any other time she would have found it crazy and extreme, but not now.

No, nothing seemed to be too extreme now.

As the days passed by, cases got worse and worse. Los Angeles shut down and nobody could come in or out of the ravished city. It had happened so fast it was dreamlike, and the hospitals were overrun with patients that never got better. They eventually began to force those who were sick to stay in their homes, a mandate that was enforced by the law. If someone in your home was stick, you had to all stay in the house together. If one person had it the others surely were infected too, and there was no use in trying to avoid the spread. They taped off your door, locked you inside, and brought you supplies as needed. It was hard to watch, and so Sarah began to actively avoid being in the house during prime news hours.

More and more neighbors became worried too, everyone was now, and Sarah and Trey noticed that others were building up supplies like their mother had. It wasn't unusual on a given day to see people going into their houses with boxes of canned goods, tents, and other supplies. Some of them even kept their cars packed at all times, as though they were living in the beginning of a zombie apocalypse film.

Out of the blue on a nondescript Tuesday, Yolanda decided that the kids could no longer visit with Darryl, and that included playing ball with him. They protested mightily, but their mother was ready with the counter offense.

"No way! His father works for the district attorney's office in Los Angeles, and they're still letting those people go to work! He could pack this home any day now, and I am not having you two catch it! No way, not happening. So you just call up your little friend and you tell him you'll see him when things are better," Yolanda had scolded them, and they knew better than to try and talk their way out of it. If she said no then no was the answer, and their father wouldn't be changing her mind.

Thus summer became a much more boring affair, since nobody else in the group was barred from seeing Darryl. That simply meant that Trey and Sarah couldn't go visit with everyone when he was around, and if they had defied their mother and she had found out things would have gotten a whole lot worse. So they had to settle for chasing the ice cream truck alone until the day it stopped making rounds, and hanging out in their own backyard. They at least had the sprinklers to run through, and a stack of comic books from the library to work on.

School was looming closer and closer though, as August began to burn quickly and they rushed towards September. Sometimes they had conversations about it; about whether or not it would be different, or if they would change things around because of Ruger. It seemed so impossible then that there would be no school, though the idea should have entered their minds by then. The virus was real, it was terrible, and it was not going anyway. Things like school had been a distant hope on the horizon ages ago, but Sarah liked to think of it as possible anyway. The routine of it, the boredom of it, would have been welcomed. Anything that was different, and anything that didn't have to do with Ruger.

It turned out that thoughts of school didn't matter, not yet, because the start date was pushed back into October. Give things time to calm down, was what the schoolboard proposed, give us time to up our cleaning regiment and figure out how to keep everyone safe. Sarah found herself disappointed, she missed school and her friends, but her mother thought it was the right decision. Safety was paramount, nothing else mattered.

Sarah let herself dream, despite knowing deep down inside that nothing would be the same anymore. Life as they knew it had ended with that pig farmer in Louisiana, and they were just starting to see the ramifications. The world was turned completely upside down, but a girl had to have hope. What is life without hope? It would have felt so much more dismal and painful, and she wanted to at least hang onto one thing. Just one, small, thing, though Ruger had other ideas. It would all get much, much worse from there, with no signs of improvement in sight.

THREE

October 2017

OVER A WEEKEND IN MID-OCTOBER, JUST A COUPLE of days before school was supposed to start, the first case cropped up in their neighborhood. It didn't come on the shoulders of Darryl's father from the district attorney's office, who was stuck in a hotel in Los Angeles with no end in sight, but rather from an elderly man named Leroy Jones. His daughter had breached the newly instated no travel ordinance to come in from Malibu to check on her father and that was all it took. One minute their little corner of the world was still relatively safe, and the next it wasn't.

They found out later that day that school, which was something that would have offered them a reprieve now from everything going on around them, was pushed back again but this time indefinitely. They had not yet worked out how to keep kids and staff safe, if they could even be safe at all, so the state thought it best if they simply postponed. Depending on the state of things in the coming weeks then they might be able to do virtual learning until students could get back into the classrooms, but as for now it wasn't looking good.

No longer allowed to visit friends and neighbors, and without the monotony of homework and reading assignments to entertain them, Sarah and Trey became bored. It was such a strange thing, to feel idle and restless when the world was crumbling, but they were. They at least had communication online with friends, which was where they found themselves spending the majority of their time.

The first to leave was Darryl himself, his entire family heading to stay with family in Malibu. They lived in a private community, locked up tight behind a gate, and he declared that he would be the safest among them until Ruger was over. Sarah quietly disagreed, because a gate didn't guarantee safety, but she didn't bother to tell him that. What good would it do to hurt his feelings and upset him? Besides that, she didn't want to make anyone mad at her. Not right now, when there might not be any time left to make any sort of amends.

It was strange to see their friends drifting away, but it became a more frequent occurrence with each passing day. Some of them left to stay with family in less populated, while others were just gone without giving an explanation. Those were the ones that bothered Sarah the most, the ones she thought about at night while laying alone in her quiet bedroom.

How did you someone you had known since kindergarten just disappear without a trace? Their social media accounts were abandoned, and text messages and emails went unanswered. It was unnerving, and one facet of Ruger that both she and Trey found it hard to reconcile with. Without school and sports and activities to hold their daily lives together, everything just felt null and void. It was hard to imagine how things would be in the coming weeks and months, as there was more and more time and many more miles between them all.

What would it be like at Halloween? Would the curfews become more strict and nobody would be allowed on the streets at all? Would there be Thanksgiving? Would there be Christmas? Neither of them could imagine life without celebrating the holiday season. There might not be any gifts or big dinners, or a live tree making the whole house smell good. Just thinking about it, about all those life altering changes, made Sarah feel more squeamish than she'd like to admit.

September limped onward, the days growing shorter and the evenings a slight bit chillier. More and more cases began to show up on the map they posted on screen during the evening news, the little red dots that signified pockets of infection growing increasingly larger by the day. Then, as October rolled in, things took a major turn. The government, it seemed, was deploying the National Guard to start locking down major cities and monitoring travel between states. They wanted to limit who was moving around the country, especially from areas with large numbers of infected.

The second the news broke things escalated from relatively calm to outright melee. Folks who hadn't yet stocked up on supplies flooded the local stores, buying up everything and anything they could get their hands on. Lines formed outside of pharmacies, grocery stores, and hardware stores, and when they ran out of supplies and locked their doors people panicked further.

They broke out windows and stormed past distraught workers, shoving each other and fighting over the few items left on the shelves whether they needed them or not.

Sarah and Trey watched it all unfold on television alongside their mother, who was on and off the phone with their father begging him to get home as fast as he could. He had left that morning to try and get to the bank, only to be stuck in long lines of traffic that moved at a snail's pace along the clogged-up highways. They could live without money for the moment, they had enough on hand, what they needed now was a plan. Something had to happen, and quick, before things got any worse.

To be perfectly honest, Sarah wasn't really sure *how* things could get much worse given the circumstances. All it had taken was one local man falling ill and things had crumbled into pieces. What would happen when it continued to spread? What would people do then? Continue to loot? Set fires? Turn on each other further? It terrified her to think that people she knew could resort to such things, and worse still that they could even take up arms against each other. These were her neighbors, her friends, the people she had grown up with and loved as dearly as she loved her own family. She never would have imagined that this sort of thing could happen, not here, and yet it was.

She hadn't ever thought much about the end of the world, but if she hadn't she wasn't sure she'd have imagined it being like this at all. This wasn't how it happened in the movies or on television shows, not at all. Programs rarely showed what happened as the world began to fall into disarray, the reality of how horrible people could truly be to one another. They usually jumped right into the action, got into the meat of what came after, but they had clearly lost out on a lot of content by not showing the breakdown. Society was faltering, badly, and nobody had ever hinted at what it might actually be like.

AUTHOR'S NOTE

Hello, beautiful readers!

I started writing this book in January of 2019, almost a year before COVID-19 came along and rocked our world. I hesitated on publication during the year of 2020, because we were living in a world that seemed far too much like the events taking place in *Transmission*. Finally though I felt okay enough to start the editing process, and when I did things felt entirely too eerie.

The things I wrote about here seemed so much more real after what happened during the initial year of the pandemic. It was sad to see the world I imagined, something I thought was only inside my mind, actually happening in the real world. I had never had that happen to me before, where my writing crossed over into my actual life, and I have to say I really hope to never have that happen again!

That being said, I hope that you enjoyed this first book in the Rag & Bone Trilogy, and that you want to join me in continuing this journey. As I write this now in 2021 the pandemic is still on-going, things are still shaky, but I do believe they will get better. For us, anyway, here in the real world. We just have to wait and see what becomes of Avery, Tilly, and the others *Ashes* (*Rag & Bone* Book 2).

See you soon!
Samantha Arthurs

SAMANTHA ARTHURS

is the author of the *Rust* series, the upcoming *Rag & Bone* trilogy, *Murder Mittens,* and *The Will*. Her debut novel, *Endless Numbered Days*, was published by Martin Sisters Publishing in 2014, and she currently works with Cat&Key Books. When not writing, she enjoys reading and reviewing books, hanging out with her dogs, playing Dungeons & Dragons, and watching horror movies. She was born and raised in Kentucky, where she still happily resides in the middle of nowhere.

Lightning Source UK Ltd.
Milton Keynes UK
UKHW040701121021
392053UK00003B/16/J